Destiny of Dreams

Time Is Dear

Destiny of Dreams
Time Is Dear

Cathy Burnham Martin

Quiet Thunder Publishing
Naples, FL   Manchester, NH   Columbus, NC

www.QTPublishing.com

This title and more are also featured at
www.GoodLiving123.com

Early Reviews & Testimonials

"Beautifully written, the type you can't put down and that you want to read to the finish, hoping it will never end. Being an Armenian, whose father and other relatives escaped the genocide, I was extremely interested, especially that it was based on truth."
-- Marian Murachanian
American Association of University Women, Clearwater

"The story was so compelling I could hardly put it down... Horrific, but true; sad, but inspiring."

-- Nancy Keller, Owner, Boston Polo Publishing Company

"Author Cathy Burnham Martin is a master at storytelling, balancing the darker and more disturbing aspects of the story with hope and positivity."   -- K.C. Finn for Readers' Favorite

"It's a story I won't soon forget. This was just a wonderous story of life, love, and determination for survival. I look forward to reading many more stories by this author."

-- Amy Shannon, Amy's Bookshelf Reviews

"You have given such an eloquent voice to their suffering, sacrifice and perseverance. Wonderful read, hard to put down, and should be a required read for high school students!"   -- Dr. David Green, Chief Medical Officer, Retired,
Concord (NH) Hospital

"Elegantly intertwined journey through time periods intersects in ways both heartbreaking and heartwarming. Two stories unified by one spirit, ***Destiny of Dreams: Time Is Dear*** is a beautiful portrayal of faith, inner strength, and dignity."
-- Indies Today

"Author Cathy Burnham Martin masterfully incorporates real-life events and people to craft a moving tale that showcases the brutal aspects of war without pulling any punches. The characters feel real, making them thoroughly compelling to read."   -- Pikasho Deka for Readers' Favorite

Destiny of Dreams
Time Is Dear

Paperback edition: ISBN 978-1-939220-57-8
eBook edition: ISBN 978-1-939220-58-5
Audiobook edition: ISBN 978-1-939220-59-2

Published and printed in the United States of America.

Library of Congress Control Number:
2021900538

Table of Contents

Glenna, Phyllis, and June - 1948

Glenna, Phyllis, and June - 1998

Dedication

With my heart filled with love, respect, and admiration, I dedicate this book to my favorite Gulumian girls.

Glenna, June & Phyllis   Glenna, Phyllis & June

My mother, Glenna Gulumian Burnham. Her twin sister, June Gulumian. Their younger sister, Phyllis Gulumian Leggett. They grew up in difficult times. They learned to be strong, and they learned to smile through it.

They taught us to respect others and ourselves. They set shining examples of family unity, church involvement, and community service. Their love shines on through everyone they have ever known. They represent our true Armenian family spirit.

Historical Note

This is a true story. It is my grandfather's story, my family's story, my story. I took the literary liberty of changing names of people still living among us as I write. As a traditional non-fiction writer, I found it natural to let real events grace the pages. More fact than fiction, I still needed to fill some gaps and build a sometimes soulfully introspective dialogue.

Further, though Armenian names can seem tricky, I let them stand. For example, Aghavni is pronounced AUV-nee. Hrant sounds like her-AUNT, with the British pronunciation of aunt. Last names ending in -ian or -yan can appear daunting. For example, Gulumian sounds like Goo-LOO-mee-an. Let them all help absorb you into the culture.

So, where does actual history stop, and the novel begin? They intertwine, although I found surprisingly little need to take wide creative freedoms, especially not with the real events. Research verified my grandfather's remembrances, both the delightful times and those more death-defying.

Despite an essential foray into 1968, timing primarily centers on the early 20th Century. Times were difficult as what later became known as World War I stirred emotions and created never-before-seen opportunities for both good and evil.

With the primary setting as the ancient walled city of Van, pronounced like the number "one" with a "v" in front of it, in the Armenian province of Van in the Ottoman Empire, you are going to my ancestors' home. These were problematic times, sadly reflecting a still-too-common disregard for people who may believe differently than we do.

My apologies for both the detailed and suggested acts of inhumanity in some of the scenes, but I cannot change, nor will I sugarcoat actual historic occurrences. No attempt was made to vilify the Ottoman Empire. However, when people live through something horrid, their eyewitness testimonies offer a distinct and memorable perspective.

I believe in the sage saying that those who forget history are destined to repeat it. My preference is to let history stand on its own. I am not here to judge. However, I do try to seek out the most positive messages I can from historic events and the people most directly impacted.

Amidst chaos in Afghanistan, the Syrian refugee crisis, and increasing firefights along the Armenian-Azerbaijan border, the importance of casting a light on intolerance and terrorism grows. Wherever we may be, we all may find ourselves on challenging journeys, with many meandering and intersecting paths. My greatest wishes are that we do all we can to become more tolerant, more loving, and more worthy people along the way.

And, as this is the story of the Armenian side of my family, we must also strive to never forget. Though this novel is historical fiction by genre, this story unfolded exactly this way. Years ago. Actually, decades ago.

Cathy Burnham Martin

Time Is Near

1

DUST SWIRLED AND dirt flew as hooves thundered down the pre-dawn road. All five horses' nostrils flared wildly as they galloped, mirroring the fierce determination of their riders.

Garabed's stallion could truly be called magnificent. As if his majestic stature was not enough, Mitan's muscular flesh radiated unequaled power. As the first rays of the morning sun oozed across the eastern sky ahead of them, his sweat-soaked midnight-black coat now glistened, his long tail extended straight out behind him, and his full mane dramatically pulsated with every step. Mitan seemed to sense the vital importance of this ride, and he inspired the other horses to keep pace, pushing their abilities to the maximum.

The riders' profiles remained low as they leaned into their steeds, literally willing them to fly these last few miles. Resolve had hardened. Their situation and troubles had grown far more dire than they had previously realized.

Rounding the bend of the final hill on their route, Garabed Gulumian knew the sadness in the news they brought home would immeasurably shake his community, family, and friends... all their lives would forever change. He now had personally witnessed brutalities he previously hoped were exaggerated.

The atrocities soared beyond his imagination. Refugees spoke of unthinkable terrors. Dozens of small children, unable to withstand the pace of a forced march, had been hurled over a cliff.

Soldiers dragged several women from their homes, stripped them naked, and hung them by the wrists in the public square. Soldiers then abused the women until they tired of having their way with their victims. An older man had horseshoes nailed onto the bottoms of his feet.

Garabed and his entourage personally saw the results of many grotesque crimes. This included finding bodies of four people who had been bound together by Ottoman soldiers and tied to a tree before being lit on fire.

The Ottomans were not just evacuating Armenians out of the six Anatolia provinces that were predominantly populated by the Christians. Oh, no. They were torturing them in the process. They were systematically wiping Armenians out.

He understood that some Muslims did not consider their acts evil. Garabed also knew they believed that when they killed an Armenian, they would go to heaven. Would God truly have mercy on the perpetrators of all these immoral and inhumane acts? Could such heinousness and hatred be forgiven?

Garabed and his father had been readying their family for weeks. Yet, he could not have imagined the horrors that were descending even now as they rode.

Regardless, they would be willing to stand their ground. They would also be prepared to flee.

Oh, how he hoped that his courier had successfully made it to the Armenian quarter in Van and delivered his note to his beloved wife, Aghavni. He pictured her touching the top of her wedding ring, where the two golden hands clasped, hiding their entwined hearts below. He knew she would be willing the men home safely, as she always did.

However, he also knew she would be completing the final tasks now. She must be. She must be readying the children. She must be ready. They all... must... be.

He shook the thoughts from his head. Garabed could not think of negative possibilities now.

With his father, Ohanes, riding at his side, Garabed re-assured himself with the knowledge that they were prepared. They were strong. They would survive. He had confidence in his family and friends.

Still, they had all hoped and prayed that the ominous situation at hand would not ever reach this unthinkable level... yet again. Barely two decades earlier, the Ottomans had driven the Armenians to the gates of Hell with the Hamidian massacres. Abdul Hamid II, the Sultan for whom the slaughters were named, wanted to unify Muslims in a fully Islamic nation. His planned slaughter of Christians wiped out hundreds of thousands of Armenians and many other Christians, too. Armenians had hoped that the times of trouble would not return so soon.

Further, the rise of the Young Turks in 1908 took away the Sultan's absolute power. Mehmed Talaat Pasha, Ismail Enver Pasha, and Ahmed Djemal Pasha, the triumvirate of the new Young Turks, had promised progressiveness and reforms. Where were these long-awaited, pledged social reforms?

None of that mattered now. There was a job to do. Bolstered by the strength of their resolve, on their steeds the men charged onward.

As they cleared the final rock outcropping, gunshots blasted the silent sky. Large boulders had shielded their view of dozens of Ottoman soldiers standing in rows blocking their path.

Turkish swords were drawn, and rifles were raised. A few officers on horseback stood to either side of the road. They all appeared as eerie silhouettes against the first rays of this cold early May morning.

The five weary horsemen came to an abrupt halt. Mitan and all the horses snorted loudly as the reins jerked, pulling them up hard. Their anxious hooves pawed repeatedly at the hard dirt.

How could this night's interruption possibly be? No one had seen Garabed and his group in Artimid. Who could have alerted the soldiers to this night's travels or their timing?

And why would the soldiers be interested in them anyway? They had run several humanitarian operations without issue, nor criticism. Quite the opposite was true. They had received official permission from the proper powers to carry out these deliveries.

Beyond the local authorities, his father's strong political connections in Constantinople had provided them clearance to carry out missions of mercy, even beyond the borders of their Van province. Officials had always expressed gratitude for all the time the respected merchant and tailor had also dedicated to calming the local political waters.

His father had served as a worthy bridge between differing political ideologies among Armenians and with the Ottomans. Why on earth would they now, suddenly, be stopped like this as they returned home?

Who, how, and why mattered very little, if at all. By name, Ohanes and Garabed Gulumian were called out! Then the soldiers gruffly ordered all the men to dismount.

The travelers did so, without hesitation. What other choice did they have?

While soldiers set about binding the five men's wrists behind their backs, one of the officers dismounted from his horse and approached them. Garabed did not recognize him. However, the icy rays of dawn did cast light on one familiar face behind the officer.

Serkan! What on earth was going on here? Serkan was Turkish, yes, but he was their friend! Still, Garabed knew that no Armenian would have ever shared their plans with Serkan Raffi. He was trusted, yes, but Armenians had learned to only trust their Turkish friends and associates to a limited point.

Then something else caught Garabed's eye. He saw something far more incomprehensible, and yet, menacing. Four long lengths of heavy rope hung from sturdy branches of two trees just to their right. Their purpose became clear as the officer approached them and started hurling accusations.

Garabed chanced a glance toward Serkan. His eyes were cast downwards. He did not look up.

Apparently, Serkan Raffi was either behind this ambush, or he knew who was. But *who* had told *any* of them of their plans? Further, how could Serkan or anyone else have known they would be returning to Van on this very morning?

Garabed barely listened to the angry drivel spewing from the young Turkish officer's mouth. They had heard all the heinous animosity spat at them many times before today. Ottoman hostility toward the Armenians reigned as legendary for generations.

So, the five men stood quietly. The yelling and shouting at them, calling them "Armenian dogs," continued. On this occasion, the insults also included vicious and utterly false accusations of revolution. Did the Ottomans now somehow believe the missions of mercy led by these tailors and merchants were, instead, meant to incite riots and revolt?

The group remained silent. They asked no questions, for they knew that they would get no answers anyway.

Suddenly, Garabed and his father were pulled away from the group. Their companions now spoke up in hurried protest.

"We are unarmed!"

"We only took clothing and food to the refugees from Vostan."

"Please let us return to our families."

"We mean you no harm, nor disrespect!"

"SILENCE!" bellowed the lead officer.

Meanwhile, soldiers completed tying separate ropes to each ankle of both Garabed and his father. The two men looked at each other most solemnly. They now knew their fates. Sadly, they had heard of this particularly grotesque, though rarely applied, Ottoman method of execution.

Garabed swallowed. He quietly said to his father, "I have been greatly honored to be your son."

"You have always made me proud," Ohanes calmly replied. "No one could hope for a son with more courage, honor, and strong character."

Before they could speak another word, the feet of both men were rudely yanked from the ground by groups of soldiers pulling on the other ends of all four ropes. The soldiers hoisted the two men, upside down, toward the branches of the trees.

Instantly, their three friends began to earnestly protest once again. The lead officer spun on them, drew his German Mauser C96 pistol, and, without hesitation, shot two of them dead.

The third, a merchant named Garin Atamian, stood stoically, waiting for the next gunshot to blast. The Ottoman officer stared at him, silently for a time.

Garin could not take his eyes off Garabed and his father, hanging by the ankles in front of him, their legs widely splayed by the distance between the ropes attached to each man's ankles. He found himself awed by the quiet calm both men exuded. Further protests were pointless. He sighed.

Garabed quietly prayed. "Sweet Jesus. Dear Lord and Holy Savior... please love and protect our family."

Now the Turkish officer directly addressed Garin. "Young man, you will live through this day, but not for many more. You. You Armenians! You pagans! You think you are all so special. You are not. So, return now to Van, your precious Armenian city. Tell your fellow heathens what happened here this morning. You and your kind are not welcome here or anywhere else. You are a blight on this earth and must be eliminated."

The officer gestured to the soldiers, standing beside the trees. One of them raised his curved Turkish saber high above his head. The officer roared, "Die, Armenian dogs!"

With that, one sword slashed downward between the splayed legs of Ohanes, the elder Gulumian. Garabed heard his father's final painful scream, as the blade nearly split his body in half. Garabed's instant grief only revealed itself in a brief, wincing gasp.

As it was raised above Garabed, the second sword glistened with a blinding reflection of the rising sun. The doomed Armenian quietly hissed at the Turkish officer, "Time is near... Time is dear."

Photo courtesy of Cesar Augusto Ramirez Vallejo

Doom
2

CASSIE SQUELCHED HER scream of horror by clasping her hand over her own mouth. She awoke in a cold sweat. That dream! Again! Every night it haunted her without mercy.

Sitting straight up in bed, the stillness of the dawn enveloped her in its icy solitude. She could not even tell if what she needed was solace or the distraction of family and friends. The usual sweat glistened over her entire body as she trembled uncontrollably. Streams of salty tears ran unchecked down her face.

Night after pain-filled night Cassie's sweet dreams had been replaced by this terror. The inescapable scenes played mercilessly over and over in her highly detailed nightmares.

The thundering hooves of the horses. The purposeful riders. The soldiers. The ambush. The glint of the long, curved sword, slicing downward as it grotesquely split the men hanging upside down. And there was so much more! Cassie wished to not fall asleep at all, because the horrifying saga merely continued.

She looked across the room at her older sister, Diana, whose sleep seemed undisturbed. Somehow, she had grown accustomed to Cassie's nightly outbursts and sobbing. To not awaken her sister, Cassie quietly slipped out of bed and sat in front of the window at one of the little desks their grandfather had built for both girls.

Cassie had changed. The free-spirited, fun-loving girl had gradually morphed into a highly troubled 13-year-old. The changes carried over into her family and school life in purely negative ways.

This all mattered not to her. The chaos of her dreams controlled everything and reigned well beyond disturbing. The images were crystal clear. Always the same. Even as the nightmare continued.

Tension. Whispered questions. And warnings. Running to find solace, sitting by the huge urn under her favorite tree in their courtyard. Staring at the brilliant blue vastness of the sky. Then shots and screams. Frantic, but futile attempts to escape. Angry eyes and hideous breath nearly suffocating her. Being dragged across the ground by her home. Her mother's plaintiff, mourning wails. Hearing her sister whimpering nearby. Flailing and shouting, trying to escape as her clothing is ripped from her body. Biting one attacker and scratching desperately at another. The gunshot ringing out.

So many vivid, but distorted depictions swirled through her mind. What did it all mean? What possible message should she ascertain from these disturbing images she endured every... single... night?

In Search of Calmness

3

THE DREARINESS OF the school day served as a welcome respite from the inevitable anguish of the night. Exhaustion utterly dashed Cassie's creativity. Her patience vanished. Straight-A grades tumbled, as she acted out in class and against her teachers.

Eighth grade was proving to be a most difficult time, socially. A physical runt and classic late-bloomer, she grew accustomed to being cruelly teased by some life-long friends. Her mother assured her that her friends did not mean it, nor did they intend her any harm.

Cassie's home situation offered no peace either. An energetic, high-spirited youth, Cassie now found herself on purely screaming terms with her parents, and she was the one doing the screaming. She flushed away all respect for herself and others. She felt only anger and deep, inexplicable sorrow.

Only later would she perhaps start to realize why all this inner turmoil had manifested. For now, surviving through another day remained her solitary goal.

Cassie felt such relief when the school day ended, and she walked toward the home of her maternal grandparents. Though barely a mile, she preferred taking a favorite shortcut along the railroad tracks. This provided what she felt was time to breathe.

No one made demands. No one gave commands. No expectations. No rules. No interference.

In fact, though she resisted admitting it, she found herself liking these afternoons very much. Cassie loved her grandparents and began looking forward to this regular time with them. They seemed to support her being herself, even when she disappointed them.

Grammy was dauntless but motherly. She could get cross, but mostly, she was a good listener. Plus, she baked wonderful cookies every day. There was nothing quite like a warm oatmeal raisin cookie or a fresh snickerdoodle or a soft, chewy sugar cookie to calm jumpy nerves.

Grampa was contemplative. He seemed more of a quiet thinker. He was never loud. In fact, Cassie could not recall a single instance where he raised his voice. She enjoyed how Grampa regularly busied himself with intricately detailed projects, from hand-making shell and enameled jewelry to various woodworking projects.

So many wonderful memories filled Cassie's thoughts. She had especially enjoyed mountain climbing with them, frolicking in the shallow water at the lake's edge where they lived, and playing on the amazingly assorted giant toys Grampa had built in her family's backyard. Her favorite had been a slide made to look just like a huge, happy giraffe nibbling grass. Cassie recalled taking a sheet of wax paper from her mother's kitchen. Sitting upon it at the top of the slide made the rapid trip down the giraffe's neck even faster.

Plus, there was the 1/3-scale model of a hand-built, 2-story Cape Cod house that he had won in a lottery at the college where he taught math. This had been the site of a great many days of fun and a good number of sleepovers with girlfriends.

All these wonderful memories and perspectives were not the reasons Cassie was here. Oh, no. Quite the opposite.

She had gotten an academic warning in Algebra. Ah, the 1960s. Cassie's parents were not impressed. She had previously been a perfect student. She had been selected for a 12-student, experimental class taking the high school Algebra course while still in junior high school. She had started with ease, but now the teacher had sent a written warning that Cassie would do well to get an average grade of C.

Her parents, Bishop and Gabrianne, were at a loss as to what to do. They had always taught their children to respect their teachers. Now Cassie had nothing good to say about her math teacher, and the teacher, not surprisingly, felt much the same about Cassie.

Neither of Cassie's parents had studied Algebra or any of this material dubbed "the new math," so neither could help her. Further, they could not afford to hire a tutor. Blessedly, Gabrianne's father had also been a math whiz. He had gone to college and earned an engineering degree. Now he was a professor of mathematics at the state technical college.

Their houses sat just two miles apart. Because Hrant Gulumian arrived home from his college academic duties by two o'clock each afternoon, and both of Cassie's parents were working, Grampa and Grammy Gulumian generously offered to be the afterschool guardians and tutors for their active, but unruly youngest granddaughter.

Cassie's parents knew the tutoring sessions would be academically helpful for her. Perhaps they intended them also as a bit of punishment, encouraging her to settle down if she wanted to return to enjoying time with her friends.

Certainly, her mother and father had been enjoying the breather of peace and calm that had resulted from the past weeks of afternoon tutoring sessions. Cassie was not raging at them and getting into more trouble.

So, it began. When school ended each afternoon, Cassie begrudgingly walked to her grandparents' home for tutoring. Bleuchk! Homework! But, again, albeit surprisingly, the stubborn lass quickly found herself looking forward to these sessions.

The Gulumian household appeared quiet and strict. A home filled with love and lessons, but not with noise and laughter. Still, Cassie and her siblings liked it. This is where they had learned to fish, swim, and boat on little Glen Lake behind the house. The lake turned out to be merely a wide section of the Piscataquog River, but it served as a wonderful lake for many families.

The siblings picked wild blueberries on the shore of Glen Lake each summer and played in the yard. Cassie especially cherished the way Grampa's thick, lush green lawn felt on her bare feet. Practicing acrobatics here proved to be most wonderful with the grass offering a forgiving mat when tumbles ended with a splat.

She also loved the calmness exuded by her grandfather as he sat in front of the smoldering coals in the fireplace. With studied patience, Hrant Gulumian turned the skewers of herbed lamb kebabs over those hot coals for what seemed like hours. Since childhood, Cassie had loved sitting at his feet, listening to his softly spoken words, and breathing in the delicious aromas of the roasting meat, onions, and herbs.

Then there were the holidays. The grandchildren never knew what to expect. One time, Grampa had built an entire miniature village beside his workshop in the basement. There were mountains and trees and a wonderful electric train that wove its way throughout it all. They could stand for hours and simply watch the train meander effortlessly through the village and countryside, even passing through a little tunnel he made in one of his mountains.

By Christmas Eve, a large, blue star always shone brightly from the peak of the roof. This was high technology for the early-1960's. Grampa had made this neon-filled star himself. He needed no D.I.Y. guides. That is good since this happened long before home computers and the Internet.

Cassie also always loved their beautiful Christmas manger scene depicting the birth of Jesus in a stable. This set-up contained real hay, a creche for the baby, with Mary and Joseph, all surrounded by animals, shepherds, and wise men. A precious angel appeared to float effortlessly at the peak of the stable. Sometimes the grandchildren got to help set up the little scene.

So many warm memories surrounded her in her grandparents' home, but Cassie was not focused on them now. Her thoughts had darkened. She felt almost totally numb.

Each afternoon was the same. She would leave school and walk to the Gulumian home. Upon arriving, Cassie dutifully sat down at the dining room table beside her grandfather.

They would speak briefly about what she had learned in school. She then reviewed that day's Algebra class and began her homework. Because she was a truly bright child, this task was completed swiftly and then checked for accuracy by Grampa.

Looking back years later, Cassie realized that she should have felt rather intimidated by her grandfather. He was a college math professor, after all. She had not given that a single thought. He was Grampa! She did not mind him checking her work one little bit.

Because there were never any errors, Hrant had started to challenge Cassie by then asking her to complete the math homework assignments he had given to his college students that day. With little or no additional instruction, she did the work swiftly and without errors.

Grampa Hrant recognized math was not Cassie's problem. She seemed to possess his mathematical abilities. Tutoring was not needed.

Something else was happening here. How he and Marjorie were going to help their animated, young granddaughter, he was not sure.

Grammy Gulumian had majored in psychology when she and Hrant met at the university. So, Marjorie's expertise might well prove more valuable than Grampa's math experience in these afternoon sessions with their frisky charge.

Goodness knows, both Marjorie and Hrant had endured challenges in their own lives that were far greater than anything to which Cassie had been exposed. They decided that she may be simply struggling with the natural changes of adolescence. She needed something to do... someone with whom she could talk.

So, after the homework session was completed each day, the three of them sat. They simply talked.

Sometimes they spoke of family activities; other times the loving grandparents shared tales of their summer road trip travels. Cassie loved the colorful map of the United States that hung upon a wall in a hallway. A different colored marking pen had been used to highlight the route followed for each trip.

Truth be told, Cassie realized that she had come to dearly love these afternoon sessions. Often, they sat on the sofas in one corner of the living room. Sometimes they stayed at the dining room table. On warm afternoons, they ventured out to the screened-in pagoda that Grampa had built in their backyard, amidst the low-bush blueberries lining the high banking of Glen Lake behind their modest ranch-style home. Wherever they sat to talk, Grammy Gulumian always brought that highly anticipated plate of homemade cookies.

Cassie cherished these conversations. She also adored seeing all the superb things he built. All their lives were filled with treasures of his skillful handiness.

In addition to that Christmas star that glowed from their roof each Christmas, Grampa had crafted electric candelabras for every window in their home. He also made them for Cassie's family home.

He had also built a large stone waterfall and pond in his backyard. The grandchildren all loved watching the multi-layered waterfall tumble into the larger pool at the bottom, which was adorned with colorful, floating flowers.

The grandchildren were mightily impressed that Grampa had built his first motorboat by hand. How they all squealed with delight watching the home movies of them all playing or riding in that boat, especially when Grampa then ran the film backward. Naturally, they enthusiastically urged him to play these segments backward again. And again. He always complied. With his charming smile.

Cassie particularly loved the summers when Grampa had constructed a series of camps around a mountain lake nearby. Once the base floors went down, he invited the grandchildren to bring sleeping bags and camp out under the stars on fun overnights. These adventures always including fishing.

Oh, and night fishing meant catching these funny-looking, bottom-feeding catfish, he called hornpout. These fish have three venomous spines on their fins, plus their long "whiskers" pack a powerful punch. Grampa never let the children remove the fish from their hooks. He required the kiddos to bait their own hooks with worms, but he always removed the caught fish, taking the bad stings for himself. He said the "ouches" became worthwhile once everyone started to chow down on these sweetly delectable fish that he fried up in a cast-iron skillet over the fire. Yummy.

Many thoughts danced in Cassie's mind. The daily conversations often revolved around these shared memories. Some of Cassie's favorite chats were about her grandmother's amazingly large collection of books. They also spoke of her grandfather's love of nature, plants, and flowers. Or family trips that found them all climbing some of the many peaks in New Hampshire's White Mountain range.

These discussions went on for weeks. Cassie stayed until her mother closed the family business office and came to pick her up. Cassie found great comfort in the home of her Grammy and Grampa Gulumian.

Since the time of her childhood naps on the sofa, she had taken comfort in the sound of their old Swiss cuckoo clock, ticking faithfully on the wall. Its constancy formed a secure sort of foundation in those otherwise silent times.

She had also enjoyed a quaint little den her grandfather built in one corner of the basement. It contained a desk and a large sofa, but otherwise, the walls were lined with dozens upon dozens of books. Biographies mostly, but also some on flowers and gardening. Grammy was an avid reader, and Grampa loved learning and doing.

Now, as a challenged young teen, Cassie did not need to escape to the quiet den and its vast array of literary volumes. Mostly, she enjoyed simply sitting and talking with her dear grandparents. Hrant and Marjorie proved to be loving sources of solace and understanding at a time when she needed it most.

Cassie's love and appreciation grew immensely for her grandparents, Hrant and Marjorie. She was too young to understand their sacrifice of time each day to help her, but Cassie relished the genuine feelings of respect she garnered from them.

Surprisingly, on one afternoon in April, life was about to change immeasurably. For them all.

Photo courtesy of Naz Israelyan

Opening the Door
4

THE CONVERSATION STARTED in its usual manner... casually. Grampa asked Cassie what she had learned in school that day. Grammy asked if anything besides her Algebra teacher had been troubling her.

Mom had shared that Cassie's nightmares seemed to be getting worse. She heard her daughter crying at night as she fought the need to sleep. Nothing seemed to calm nor comfort the girl. Marjorie knew that many different triggers could cause stress, nightmares, and sleep loss. They all wondered what on earth could possibly be tormenting this girl.

Cassie had never mentioned her recurring dreams to her grandparents. All she had even told her parents was that she was having bad dreams. Cassie thought the dreams' content to be irrelevant to her real life. Or perhaps she was avoiding confronting the subject altogether because it terrified her so deeply.

But, hey! This was another afternoon to chat with her beloved grandparents. Though these visits only lasted 2-3 hours, for Cassie, it was as if time stood still. She felt beautifully alive here.

Today, however, Cassie started nervously prattling on and on about nothing... and anything. She appeared highly distracted. And yet, she remained unaware that her grandparents now knew of her dreams' existence.

Marjorie gently placed her hand on one of Cassie's hands. Cassie stopped chatting instantly. She quizzically looked at her grandmother.

Marjorie calmly said, "No. We are not going to talk about any of that today. Your mother says you had nightmares again last night. So, today, we would like to start to talk about them. Is that okay?"

Hesitating, Cassie cast a worried look at her grandmother. "I guess so," she finally replied. She was not sure she wanted to talk about these dreams at all. In fact, during the daytime, she actively attempted to think of anything *but* the nightmares.

"Don't worry," Grammy continued. "You are very safe here. We hope you know that. So, tell me, Cassie. Do you feel safe now, here with Grampa and me?"

"Oh, yes," Cassie said, without hesitation.

Grammy nodded. Her typically firm-set jaw seemed soft and comfortable. "We did not know you were having nightmares. Just start by telling us what happens. What do you see in these dreams?"

Cassie paused. "Well, there are the horses. Most of them look golden, but one is shiny and black."

"That's good," Marjorie softly responded. Her eyes were warm and encouraging. However, she knew horses did not constitute bad dreams.

"What else do you see when you see the horses?" Marjorie and Hrant sat still as they awaited Cassie's next reply.

Cassie took a deep breath. Then she launched into detailed descriptions of the male riders and the strange garb they wore. She told of the open countryside, the hills, the trees, and the rocky terrain. Her eyes moistened as she described the shock of the ambush, the shouting, the anger, two men getting shot. Then sobs and tears ran unchecked.

"Perhaps this is enough for today," Marjorie suggested. Cassie, still holding her grandmother's hand, squeezed firmly.

"Nooooo," she managed, though her throat had tightened with terror. She could not open this door without stepping through it.

She continued. "There is much more!"

The silence in the room was cracked only by Cassie's hard breathing, measured by the regular ticking of the old cuckoo clock hanging on the wall behind them. Finally, Cassie was ready to speak again.

Initially, she backtracked, talking again about the horses, noting the beauty of the huge black horse being the finest in the stable. She explained how he was considered a truly treasured stallion.

She'd had the dream so many times. This reigned as one of those rare dreams in which she could recall every detail.

Cassie proceeded to tell of the steep hillsides and the wide-spreading plateau. She told of the beautiful, 2-story house with balconies. In her dream, this was her home, in which she lived with her family, though they were not the same family as in real life.

Still, she seemed to know various people and described them and the home's details. The courtyard. The large, colorful urn. Her favorite mulberry tree.

Cassie described the landscape and hillsides, and a huge nearby lake that was like an ocean. The massive snow-topped mountain in the distance and the craggy cliff and ancient castle directly behind them. The neighborhood, the town square, "her dream parents," and "dream grandfather."

None of this was the scary part. Marjorie thought the description perhaps simply reflected a fantasy escape. However, Cassie's grandmother also knew her granddaughter had merely set the stage.

The awful thing was, no matter how many times she'd had the dream, Cassie explained that she couldn't change the ending. In other dreams in the past, she had always been able to do just that. She knew she could simply fall back to sleep and redirect the dream to a better conclusion. But not this dream. No matter how hard she tried.

Her grandmother gently prodded and encouraged her for details about what was happening in these dreams that upset her so much. Cassie faltered. She had shared the easy stuff. The descriptions.

Now she slowly began to divulge the peculiar tale of this favorite black horse. He was carrying a man she knew, who was unwittingly leading the group of men into one horrific ambush.

The other awful men on horseback, with those massive, curved swords, were killing people. The soldiers shouting. The rifles. The brandished swords. The two men being strung up by their ankles. The flash of the hideous sabers as they sliced the two men nearly in half.

The dream absolutely terrified her. Cassie was crying hard by the time she had finished telling them of the ambush.

Her grandfather remained utterly quiet, but soon he gently spoke. He now asked her a few questions, which she answered. Then he started to talk, telling of things that even Grammy had never before heard him share.

Hrant did not know how the information arrived in his little granddaughter's brain... how she knew of these things... how she saw such specific elements. She was describing the area around his childhood home in Van, Armenia.

In her dream, she had seen his father and grandfather. Cassie even knew his Papa's precious horse, Mitan.

When the Ottomans set out to obliterate Armenia, determined to eliminate the race, the bloodshed had indeed been horrific. She did not consciously know anything about any of these things. And yet, how was she accurately detailing such a specific and accurate event?

Young Cassie somehow knew it all. And it did not stop there. She then relayed how the torturous dreams continued.

Armenian moon
Photo courtesy of Cesar Augusto Ramirez Vallejo

Providence
5

SHARING MORE OF the recurring dream, Cassie saw those same two ill-fated men, but this time in a household. She felt comfortable and safe in this dream home, though it also seemed somehow otherworldly.

Regardless, she knew every inch, every nook and cranny, including where she had hidden some of her books, in a vegetable cellar. She explained being puzzled as to why she and her dream sister hid books amongst the vegetables, but they did so.

Marjorie urged her to simply share, with no worries. Cassie further described the peculiar, boxy 2-story architecture and the large walled courtyard in the back with its little orchard and some grapevines. There were stables on one side and a big, but odd oven-like structure at the back of the yard.

Behind the house rose an immense rocky precipice near the house with a massive, ancient-looking castle or fortress on top. She also spoke again of the nearby expansive lake, so large it appeared more like a sea.

In part of the dream music and dancing filled the night air. Many people were gathered. Lots of candles flickered brightly, causing fun shapes of light to flit across the brightly colored outfits worn by all the people in attendance. She and another female, who seemed to be her older sister, were doing a lot of giggling. A darling little boy danced tirelessly on the tabletop. Everyone cheered and clapped their hands.

Then it grew dark. Tears flowed as Cassie described hearing the whispers and warnings. Then the men were all gone. There remained no music, no dancing, no laughter.

An urgent knock at the door was followed by frantic conversation... then painful wailing. A man told of what had just happened at the ambush.

Then Cassie explained how she somehow felt herself rushing to her favorite mulberry tree in the walled back courtyard for solace. Others huddled together in a corner inside the house before the unthinkable happened.

The outer door had crashed open. Many angry men in uniforms burst through it and into their home.

A woman jumped up in protest, but one of the men backhanded her... hard... driving her to the floor. So much yelling filled the air.

Men grabbed a teenaged girl, not much older than Cassie, and dragged her into the courtyard. They then spied Cassie. Several of the men stormed toward her.

Tears ran down Cassie's face freely now as she described the ensuing nightmarish details from a perspective as if she had left her body and watched from mid-air. Terror flashed across her face now. She paused briefly and then continued.

She watched herself flail and fight, uselessly, as one man scooped her up off the ground beside her urn. They were taking her away! Cassie wailed, "Noooo!"

She pounded and scratched at the back of the man who had flung her over his shoulder. Another man then started pulling at her. Suddenly, amidst the yelling, things got worse.

Cassie saw herself battling now as men ripped away her clothing and beat her. The older woman who had tried to intervene earlier rose again. As she attempted to rush through the door to the courtyard, she shouted and clawed at the men. This time, when they flung her to the floor, one of the men then slammed the butt of his rifle down hard on her left hand, completely smashing her fingers.

Still, she defiantly rose again, fiercely commanding the men to release them and leave their home. Though soldiers now held the woman back, she continued urging the two girls to stay strong.

"Just survive this," she urged vehemently. "Survive!"

Soldiers knocked the woman down again. One of them then ground the heel of his boot into her already bleeding hand. Two others now held her down. She could not rise again.

Meanwhile, men pinned Cassie and the older teen to the ground, while others repeatedly attacked the two young girls. Cassie saw the other teen, who appeared to be just two or three years older than she, gazing at her, with complete resignation in her eyes.

"Oh, no!" Cassie thought. "She was giving up."

In sharing the dream, Cassie described the older girl's calmness. She saw her just quietly weeping as she was brutally savaged. Her eyes simply stared, with an odd sort of blank desperation.

Cassie would have no part in giving up. She fought as mightily as she could. No match for the soldiers, at the end of the attack, she continued to scream at the men... even as she saw the pistol drawn and pointed directly at her.

Bang! And then nothingness.

Cassie would wake up. It was over. Again.

Sitting safely in the Gulumian home, Cassie's sobs soaked her grandmother's shoulder. Marjorie hugged her grandchild to her, wishing she could somehow ease this horrific pain. Her granddaughter was describing acts for which the youth did not even yet have words.

Through it all, Hrant and Marjorie listened quietly. They watched the steady tears flow down their granddaughter's cheeks as she shared the more painful scenes her dreams brought to her every night. Marjorie now gently held Cassie's trembling hand.

They sat quietly for a time after Cassie finished telling the dream's dreadful details. Concern clouded Marjorie's gaze.

These were far from normal images for a young American girl in the 1960's. No movies. No books. Nothing she knew of had such a terrifying tale. What could cause Cassie to be seeing such horrible images?

Marjorie continued to hold and gently rock her sobbing grandchild. She reassured her, "You are safe now. You are safe. You are loved. Everything is all right."

Finally, Cassie grew quiet. She always eventually stopped shaking after waking from these dreams. Every night.

Soon Cassie spoke again. "Sorry, it all sounds crazy, I know. Maybe I'm just losing my mind."

"No," Marjorie cooed. "You are just having a troubled time. These are dreams, my dear. They are highly disturbing dreams, but they are just dreams."

Hrant, who had remained silent since Cassie started to reveal the dream's details, began to open up. She had described his childhood home in Armenia. Cassie perfectly detailed the house, their neighborhood, and the massive lake. She even knew where his sisters had hidden their books. As the Ottoman Empire did not encourage girls to read or have books, they hid their books, to avoid getting caught by the officials during a random inspection for weapons and ammunition. In his characteristically calm manner, Hrant slowly reached over and took Cassie's other hand in both of his.

She looked up into his soft, dark eyes. Ever-so-gently, and thoughtfully, he slowly began to speak.

"You are not at all crazy, Cassie. In fact, these may *not* be just dreams."

Marjorie and Cassie both looked at him quizzically. Cassie asked, "What do you mean, Grampa?"

Hrant looked at Cassie. Then he looked at his wife. Looking back at Cassie, he softly began to speak.

"I have never been a particularly religious man, but I have strong faith. I sometimes seem to have more questions than answers. For example, I am not sure how best to say this. I don't know if there *is* such a thing as reincarnation, but..."

Hrant paused. He now gently placed both hands on either side of Cassie's face. Then, in his matter of fact, but still soft-spoken way, he said, "If there *is* such a thing as reincarnation, I believe you were one of my sisters in Armenia."

The monastery at Khor Varap
with Mount Ararat in the background.
Photo courtesy of Makalu

Deeply Hidden Memories

6

COMPLETE SILENCE SETTLED across the room. In shock, Cassie stared into her grandfather's eyes. He revealed nothing more in his gaze. She looked to her grandmother. Marjorie's jaw had dropped. Even she had not been prepared for what her husband had just said.

Since they first met at the University of New Hampshire in the 1920s, he had never once spoken of his life in Armenia. She knew that Turkish troubles had brought him and his family to America. She knew his mother and older brothers, all of whom had been most helpful to them. She knew that life had been extremely difficult for them.

Yet, Hrant had never offered any other details. Not once would he speak of it, even when she had tried to ask questions. The ambush? Sisters? Attacks?

Oh, sure. There were rumors. Marjorie recalled as a child having heard the adults speak of an occasional news report. These had told of mostly women, children, and elderly Armenians being walked many miles from their homes and towns, often with no food nor water. They had sometimes been stripped naked, and all their possessions had been stolen by their Ottoman guards.

Most died of exposure or starvation on these forced marches to and through Syrian deserts. Thus, phrases like "the starving Armenians" and "the suffering Armenians" evolved in these dark days... and years.

Marjorie was right. At the time the events had happened, various newspaper reports recounted incidents where dozens or hundreds or even thousands of bodies of Armenians had been found. The people had been sometimes shot. More often than not, they had been savagely stabbed and even chopped at with sabers. Their lifeless bodies were left in rotting mounds.

Sometimes, someone left still barely alive had managed to crawl their way out from under the carnage. They survived to reveal the horrific truth about what the Ottoman Empire was doing to its Armenian people.

Journalist and missionary records reflected many previously untold horrors. Yet, these accounts had initially appeared to be isolated. Regardless, leading nations of the free world repeatedly called on Ottoman leaders to stop the escalating and brutally systematic attacks.

Marjorie, as with other United States children during those times, would know little, if anything, about these activities. Parents isolated children from awareness of such experiences, protecting them as much as possible from unthinkably disturbing news.

To make matters of information even more challenging, the news of what was happening to Armenians at the hands of the Ottoman Turks came out publicly with infrequency. For Americans, particularly, these events were taking place in lands that were highly unknown to them.

Missionaries, government liaisons, and foreign military personnel directly witnessed many brutalities. Unfortunately, the atrocious acts perpetrated against the

Armenians were not at all rare, nor isolated. Written records sadly documented a great many atrocities.

Eyewitnesses wondered just how many *more* had occurred without witnesses to reveal the truth or hold the Ottomans accountable later. They shuddered to imagine.

Indeed, following the Great War, the Young Turks' leaders would be found guilty of countless human atrocities and their deliberate and calculated plan to annihilate all Armenians. They would be ordered to return the lands to the Armenians and restore their confiscated property, belongings, and wealth.

Though it would come very much after the fact, the acknowledgment was important. The world knew the truth and had spoken up for what was right.

Unfortunately, as the world got busy with other pressing matters, no one monitored what the new Turkish republic did, or, more specifically, what they failed to do. They made no reparations to the Armenian people. Quite the opposite occurred.

Though seemingly impossible, additional massacres took place, while the new Turkish leadership actively set out to erase evidence of all things Armenian, regardless of their thousands of years of well-storied past. This "Turkification" included changing names of towns, rivers, buildings, monuments, and anything else that bore Armenian names or origins.

This meant destroying records reflecting Armenian artists, sculptors, designers, architects, and more. They changed names to reflect Turkish names to be sure no credit would ever be given to anyone Armenian.

They also destroyed records of Armenian births, education, and citizenship, not to mention property and business ownership. The new Turkish government even ordered the demolition of a great many towns and churches. A "great many" translates here into many hundreds.

They moved Muslim Turks into remaining Armenian homes and gave them ownership. The word "Armenia" and all Armenian words were stricken or changed on all maps, books, and documents.

Until she met Hrant, Marjorie had never met someone who had been there in person. She merely knew his family's troubles were very bad, and the perpetrators had been Ottoman Turks.

Now, in the 1960s, Cassie knew nothing of Armenia or Turkish troubles. Mass media and the World Wide Web remained decades away.

And yet, her Armenian grandfather had just said he believed that Cassie could have been his sister in a former life. The girl thought of how to respond. In truth, she barely knew what the word "reincarnation" indicated.

Then, without really knowing where she found the words, Cassie heard herself quietly reply. "Well, if I am your sister, I am having a much better life this time around."

Marjorie looked at the loving, but pained expression on Hrant's face as he gazed into Cassie's still tear-swollen eyes. Her compassion for her husband, this gentle, hard-working, and highly intelligent man, quadrupled as he now began recounting his childhood steps.

The Historic Stage
7

"YEYYYYY!!!" THE MEN pounded on the tables with great glee. Celebration resounded! Aghavni smiled at her husband and his father, surrounded by their many friends. Garabed reveled in his glory.

Aghavni and the other ladies brought out more platters of kebabs, perfectly browned by the men over the slow coals. They surrounded the meats with rounds of cracker bread and roasted onions. They also brought an abundant supply of various side dishes, plus figs, dates, raisins, and dried peaches and apricots, all harvested during the previous season.

How deeply she enjoyed seeing the tables lush with foods, and their menfolk relaxing and enjoying each other. They had not always been able to do so.

Times had turned into such difficulty and despair just 20 years earlier. Ottoman Turkish sentiments had railed against the Armenians. This behavior became a far-too-frequent recurrence for the Armenians. Many lives were lost, including that of the elder Ara Samargian, Aghavni's paternal grandfather, in one skirmish. Plus, her mother-in-law was killed along with a group of other ladies, simply for being in the wrong place at the wrong time. It seemed the painful torment would never end.

Chaos had eventually settled into calmness once again, and the Ottoman Turks let the Armenians return to a semblance of normalcy. The Gulumians knew life would never be truly normal. It had not been so in too many decades. Centuries, even. Yet, the Armenians prevailed. This is part of the Armenian way. Each generation was dutifully taught to always do the best possible... to always persevere, despite obstacles and challenges.

Trouble was no stranger. Their Armenian ancestors had lived around Lake Van at the base of Mount Ararat in the Caucasus Mountains region since around 2,000 BC. Many empires had come and gone. The fertile soils bridging Europe with the Far East along the famed "Silk Road" stirred powerful stronghold desires for every rising empire.

Periodic loss of independence marked Armenia's thousands of years of history during occupations by Persians, Greeks, Romans, Byzantines, Mongols, Arabs, and, finally, the Ottoman Turks. Though the Ottoman Empire had conquered Armenia in the 16th Century, even they continued to call the region Armenia, until, that is, following the Great War, which later became named World War I.

We humans can be most interesting. We can sometimes lull ourselves into believing that if we deny, ignore, rewrite, or attempt to blot out portions of our history in books or records or even verbal discussions that these historic events somehow never happened. Sigh. We can believe what we want, but it does not change the truth.

The Armenians had survived attempted obliteration and oppression multiple times and managed to maintain their nationality and spirit. Their Christian faith sparked problems throughout the region. This was far from new.

They knew that the Armenian King Tiridates III declared Christianity to be the official Armenian religion around 300 AD. This made the Armenian Kingdom the first Christian nation in the world.

None of the neighboring nations ever followed suit. Unfortunately, some regimes began to loathe the Armenians for their faith. Centuries later, Armenia, locked within the Ottoman Empire, remained the region's only Christian nation.

Armenians had long been despised for it or at least distrusted. Systematic persecution within the Ottoman Empire became expected. All that hatred served only to strengthen the Armenian resolve.

A peace-loving people, many Armenians appeared to accept their subservient position. Then again, what else could they do? They were considered citizens. However, the Ottomans most assuredly thought of Armenians as less than second-class in status. Armenians were merely expected to assist, support, and help Turkish people whenever needed or called upon to do so.

Because the Turkish Sultan did not want his people having to associate with the Armenians any more than was absolutely necessary, however, he had required Christians to maintain separate schools, businesses, and such. He also authorized the levying of severe additional taxes on all Armenian citizens, for the simple reason that they were Armenians. These poll taxes applied to all non-Islamic groups within the Ottoman Empire territories, specifically Jews, Armenians, and other Christians from Greeks and Serbs to Bulgarians and Assyrians.

Regardless of the pressures applied, Armenians persevered. A small, but hearty nation of people, they took great pride in their faith, family, and rich heritage. Even for women, they encouraged higher education and cultural development, still highly discouraged or even unthinkable in the Islamic society surrounding them.

Armenians drew strength from collaborations. Everyone worked, although the Ottoman Empire's laws forbade women from working outside the home. Armenians were also active in their communities, although laws prevented them from holding most government posts or serving on juries sitting in judgment of Turks.

They also seemed to toil longer and harder than their fellow Turkish citizens, muchly because a powerful work ethic had always been a building block in the Armenian family foundation. They did not complain. Simply because it was the right thing to do, everyone worked hard, and everyone enjoyed the bounty.

Sadly, this set the Armenians up to be on the receiving end of a great deal of jealousy. Assuredly, they worked hard and chose to save whatever money they could, despite their special higher taxes. Many Turks did not see the Armenians' frugality as a positive trait. Instead, resentment festered and grew, as Armenians were viewed as unfairly wealthy.

At this time, the deep history provided a solid base for the Gulumian family. Although the social situation appeared stable on the surface, quiet grumblings and shifting attitudes signaled both hope and insecurity.

However, on this night, such concerns and thoughts were set aside. They feasted in both celebration and farewell. Their second son, Aram, was heading to America. He would be joining their first-born son,

Ohanes, who had been named after Garabed's father in the Armenian tradition.

Aram would finally get to study to become either a teacher or perhaps a doctor. Teaching had always been a passion and his avocation for a couple of years. And yet, his friends had long ago nicknamed him "Doc." They often said he possessed a scholarly, analytical approach to life.

Though Aghavni and Garabed enjoyed many Turkish friends, none were in attendance on this particular evening. Such friendships had to be carefully guarded and kept secret from most of the Ottoman leaders. If certain people learned of these cross-cultural relationships, disapproval would be the least of anyone's worries. Penalties could be fierce and social repercussions would be inevitable.

Further, grumblings had surfaced of a potential war brewing in Europe. The Ottoman Empire was thought to be empathizing with Germany. America and the rest of the free world looked down on Turkey's apparent budding alliance with the Germans. Further, any war would bode poorly for travel abroad, and many Armenians were actively trying to move adult children to America.

Other risks crossed all their minds. Just two months earlier, a grand and new steamship bound for America had struck an iceberg and sunk. Some 1500 people had perished on the ballyhooed maiden voyage of the Titanic. The family wiped such thoughts from their minds.

Thanks to his father's strong political ties, Garabed had secured trans-Atlantic passage for his son. Aram's travel and studies in the United States had been approved by the Sultan himself.

A high-ranking Turkish family friend then arranged for Aram to travel with a group going on a consulate trip to the U.S.A. This meant that he could travel in nice accommodations rather than in the crowded lower decks, though the Ottomans were unlikely to condone that. Indeed, his papers showed Aram was booked in steerage aboard the Martha Washington, which would set sail for America from the port of Patras on the island of Crete.

Interestingly, the family learned that the Turkish group he traveled with intended to serve up false assurances in the West regarding any intentions they may have of going to war on the side of Germany. Their Turkish friends shared with the Gulumians that the Ottoman leaders had liked the idea of adding an Armenian to their group, as it would make Turkey appear more fair-minded, well-intentioned, and credible to the American government.

The Gulumian family did not care about political pretenses. They cared even less to be unwittingly made a part of the Ottoman scheme to falsely reassure the United States regarding their intentions to side with Germany against the rest of Europe.

In America, the eldest son had already addressed this with his resistance contacts. Serving as an elementary school teacher in Van, Aram had received approval to travel to the United States to further his education. They would not let the Turks interfere with what was supposed to happen. They would be in New York City with the younger Ohanes and an American government official when the Martha Washington arrived, to help safely remove Aram from the group. The Ottomans could not use their political might against him once he cleared Ellis Island and traveled to Boston.

He would then finish his education and work with organizations to help other Armenians. The Ottoman political climate would then determine if he would return to Armenia or seek refuge in the U.S.A. Aram had also let his older brother know that he would gladly sign up to serve in the U.S. Army, though he had vowed that he would not fight for the Ottoman Empire nor the Sultan for even one single day.

Aram was grateful for his father and grandfather. Garabed and the elder Ohanes remained as active in government as they were permitted. They were well-respected, both within the Armenian quarters of Van and within Turkish circles. As a distinguished businessman and tradesman, his father had also cultivated a great many valuable and well-connected contacts in Constantinople.

As merchant tradesmen and tailors by trade, his family had always enjoyed the company of a great many Armenian leaders as well. Tonight's celebration presented no exception. A veritable Armenian "Who's Who" sat in attendance.

The family had hosted them in this very courtyard multiple times. Some were close friends, like the money changer Grigor Terlemezian and his sister-in-law, Hulianna, a dear friend of Aghavni. Others were neighborhood families, including a favorite teacher Krikor Yesayan, a couple of local newspaper editors, and merchant friends Atamian and Kherbekian. It was the second Kherbekian son, Toros, who was betrothed to marry the delicate Nazeli, Aram's sister, when she turned 17 years of age in just two years.

Politics remained unavoidable in their circles, so activists and leaders always topped the guest lists. Tonight's attendees included Amenak Hovan, Armenian National Assembly member Harutiun Yangülian, the noted revolutionary statesman Aram Manukian, along with the celebrated Armenian hero, Dajad Terlemezian, son of Aghavni's best friend, Hulianna.

A couple of trusted priests from the monastery also attended, as usual, as well as their favorite minstrel. He just happened to be the son of a most highly respected priest from the Cathedral of the Holy Cross on Akhtamar Island.

The music reflected everyone's upbeat mood. This night's purpose focused on celebration. Friends and neighbors called out, "Aram, we will miss you!"

"Aram, we wish *we* were going *with* you!" Laughter lilted over the gathering.

"Come on, Doc. Tell us again about your trip."

He waved them off, as usual. Aram was a man of few words. In America, he would further his studies. And he could continue to work on his passion for art. In truth, if he could have his way, he would study art, rather than teaching or medicine. But the time for playing had passed. He had to set his sketching aside.

Aram was not particularly talented in musical arts, which was peculiar for a Gulumian. He appreciated it greatly, to be sure. However, the visual arts had captured his heart. His talent for depicting shadows and reflections of light received great praise.

Now, over the music, Aram started to hear an encouraging and familiar chant. "Hrant! Hrant! Hrant! Hrant!"

The friends knew they were not going to get Aram to stand up and give a speech. So, now they called the name of his youngest brother.

This was far from the first time the youngster had been summoned to center stage. It seemed that at every gathering since Hrant could walk, he would end up singing and dancing on the tabletop, pleasing Aram and everyone else in the family.

As usual, his father hoisted the little lad up onto the table. Trays and dishes had been hastily cleared by Aghavni, Hulianna, and his two sisters.

"Thank you, Aghavni," Garabed had said, gently touching her arm as she passed by. As always, she smiled at his regular acknowledgment of her efforts, even as the musicians immediately segued into a popular folk song.

Hrant grinned. Ah, yes. He smiled his precious, contagious smile. It lit up his entire face and crinkled his deeply hazel, almond-shaped eyes.

He immediately started his sure-footed dancing. Hrant was confidently stepping and leaping back and forth. His kicks were high, and his eyes twinkled with his usual confidence and glee.

Soon many of the guests had linked pinky fingers and were circling. They celebrated with traditional Armenian folk dancing, topping off a delightful evening.

These were among the many happy memories they would always cherish. Family. Harvest. Laughter. Music. Their parents' sparkling eyes.

Everyone cheered. On this night, Aram received a warm and wonderful send-off. Somber talk, survival planning, and resistance training would all continue another day. For now, little Hrant represented the powerful hope they all needed so very deeply.

Cathedral of the Holy Cross
on Akhtamar Island in Lake Van
Photo courtesy of Olia Nayda

The Gardens

8

HRANT LOVED SUMMER. Lake Van stretched out like a vast ocean in the highlands between the Armenian provinces of Van and Bitlis. It was the biggest ocean he had ever seen. He learned it was more than 600,000 years old with its long row of mountains to its north formed by volcanoes.

The hills around the lake rolled gently, covered with glorious orchards and vineyards. While here, they enjoyed abundant harvests of pears, apricots, olives, grapes, and much more. Laughter and music, family and fun-filled endless days and nights.

They never came to the summer house during the winter. Of course, the winter temperatures here in the Western Asia highlands averaged just 26 degrees Fahrenheit. Summers, however, were merely marvelous. Everything bloomed with temperatures averaging a sweet 72 degrees.

Hrant could not recall hearing how or when his family had acquired the vineyards and the summer house by Lake Van. It seemed they had always owned this home. Regardless, he loved his memories of their times there. These thoughts gave him comfort throughout his life.

The days felt long and carefree around the gardens. He and his siblings ran gleefully through the vineyards and fruit trees. They would bob and weave, play hide-and-seek, and munch on whatever delicious fruits they desired. Loud, colorful buntings and warblers in the almond trees and orchards provided constant entertainment.

Hrant also learned to swim at Lake Van. The waters were very salty, and some places were called brackish. Those were not fit for swimming, so they avoided them, opting instead for the areas where freshwater constantly flowed into the lake. But he did love being in the water. Swimming brought him relaxation and peace.

He became fascinated with life around the water, in general. Hrant particularly enjoyed the many boats, both small ones and the larger merchant and ferry vessels. He often thought that he would one day have a boat of his own.

Though he was quite certain that no such beast existed, he also found himself keeping watch for the so-called Lake Van Monster. Hrant heard that an Ottoman newspaper had chronicled the story of a creature coming out of Lake Van in the late 1800s and dragging a man back into the water.

Scientists had not ever been able to find nor see the monster. Still, Hrant could not help but wonder if there might be some peculiar descendent of an old mythological Armenian dragon lurking about the lake.

He had heard about a dragon that would come out and devour any other Vishaps or dragons that had grown large enough to devour the world. It was rumored that the beast was brown and scaly, some 30-40 feet long, with big side flippers and a long, reptilian face. Hrant's eyes widened as some said it closely resembled the extinct Mosasaurus or even a whale-like Basilosaurus. A typical boy, he thought finding this animal would be marvelous! But this was fantasy.

In reality, watching the wide array of birds added a special, everyday fascination for the young lad. Around the house in Van, he saw some large storks and lots of that long-beaked butterscotch-colored bird with sharp, black-striped wings and a tuft on his head. That was the Eurasian hoopoe, a very common bird.

So, Hrant fancied the birds he only got to see at the summer house. He often commented on the large herons, pelicans, and swans that entertained him as he sat at the water's edge whittling some new wooden toy or flute.

He particularly liked the big pink and white birds that he learned were called flamingos. They often frolicked in the shallow waters, so he could see them up close. Plus, the many funny-looking, white-headed ducks with blue-colored bills always made him smile.

At night, he loved sleeping under the stars on the rooftop. The air smelled so much sweeter here. The summer breezes tickled his skin. He enjoyed resting there and listening to the silence of the countryside.

Though they were not far outside the walls of Van, the city sounds vanished completely. Here he only heard the rustling of the leaves of the many trees, the chirping of a wide variety of birds, and sometimes, particularly on windy days, even the sounds of the surf pounding the nearby shore.

He looked up at the moon. Hrant especially treasured the nights when the full moon appeared to have grown so large that he thought it might swallow the earth. Then, of course, he loved the starlight. Stars also captured his imagination. He thought his favorite constellation of all was perhaps Leo, the lion.

He especially loved the evenings when the whole family slept on top of the roof. His sister, Anush, always wove wonderful tales of the ancient heroes slaying the demons, all depicted in the constellations.

Mama stayed with them at the summer house all the time. On the weekends, Hrant's Papa and Grampa returned from working in the city. They brought with them lots of sewing work for his mother and sisters to do.

Various friends visited them at the summer house, too, along with their families. There were always lots of friends with whom to share daily adventures. These were the best days. However, Hrant lamented that these delightfully fun times somehow seemed to pass too quickly.

The evenings also overflowed with festivity. Large trays were abundantly piled with the most intriguing arrays of food, with plenty of khorovats, the aromatic, perfectly charred skewers of meat that had been grilled over open flames. Much revelry and game playing followed. As usual, the telling of grand stories captured Hrant's attention. And the merriment of music sparkled as his favorite time.

When guests played their music and sang, the men regularly lifted the youngest Gulumian boy onto the table, encouraging him to dance and sing. He needed no encouragement. As usual, dance he did, leaping fearlessly into the air and relishing all the cheers from the onlookers.

These cherished memories kept Hrant's spirit alive in the darkest times. Every year since he could remember held something special from their days at the summer home in the gardens.

He especially recalled a morning they all boarded a couple of large boats on Lake Van. These delivered them to an island in the south part of the lake.

Hrant remembered being intrigued by a great castle that had been built at the water's edge there. Although now it was totally underwater due to the lake level rising, everyone could clearly see the castle's details through the crystal waters.

On this day, they attended a big wedding ceremony at a large church on a hill there. Hrant believed this church hailed from medieval times. He remembered it as very impressive. Indeed, the Cathedral of the Holy Cross on Akhtamar Island shone as so remarkable that it would become one of very few monasteries and churches spared from destruction by the Ottomans following their defeat in the Great War.

As impressive as the church was for Hrant, he was equally taken in by what seemed to be the inordinate length of the wedding service. While it likely lasted merely one hour, it felt much longer for the young lad. Father Der Hagopian performed the marriage rituals with his classic flair.

Hrant lacked the maturity to appreciate the pompous ceremony. The young boy struggled to focus. He found himself counting the many shimmering candles to help pass the time.

Hrant looked around a lot, too. He liked the white, green, and red ribbons woven through the crowns for the bride and groom. He looked forward to seeing the crowns placed on the bridal couple's heads, signifying their newly formed little kingdom. Aghavni had explained to him that the white stood for peace, the green represented life, and the red signified sacrifice.

Everyone in attendance exuded happiness. They were all dressed in their finest clothing. Since his family overflowed with renowned tailors, Hrant saw many garments fashioned by the Gulumians. Beyond well-tailored suits, all sorts of colorful garb could be seen on this day. Even the guests' shoes sparkled in many colors.

He also admired the handiwork of his sisters. Both Nazeli and Anush had beautifully embroidered the detailed stitchery that embellished countless shirt collars, jackets, vests, and skirts that now surrounded him on the wedding attendees.

Not to mention the bride's gown. He had observed the women in the house laboring for a great many evenings, creating an abundance of lace and fancy appliques and trims that inspired "oohs" and "ahhs" as soon as the bride entered the sanctuary.

Regardless, the thrill and entertainment value of all that had worn off for the young lad. Hrant now craned his neck as he twisted in his seat to turn and look at everyone around them. Yet again, he needed something else to capture his attention.

Suddenly, he felt his mother's stern gaze upon him. Hrant ever... so... slowly... turned his face toward her. Aghavni subtly but firmly shook her head. He immediately sat straight up, facing forward. He folded his hands on his lap.

Sigh. Perhaps he simply wanted to get to the party that was promised to follow. Preparations at the house had been going on for what seemed like weeks.

Finally, after what felt like hours to the little lad, it was time to get on the big boat and head back to the mainland. Hrant thoroughly enjoyed riding on this huge boat. He was not sure that the boat he might want to own one day needed to be like this. Certainly not this large, naturally, but a boat all his own.

After reaching the shore, a collection of horse-drawn carriages awaited to transport the guests. Everyone gathered at the Gulumian summer home near the lake for the post-wedding celebration.

As the sun prepared to set, people lit many lanterns and torches. The grounds looked spectacular! Hrant felt as if he was at a festival. Was this really his house?

He heard the piercing woodwind sound of the zurna instrument and the delightful pounding of the kopal, a large, double-headed drum. Colorful banners filled the yard. Minstrels, musicians, friends, and neighbors flowed in through the vineyards. As the crowd grew, it seemed there must be at least two hundred people there. This became the biggest party Hrant had ever seen!

He did not even know who had gotten married, but his family was very much involved in hosting the event. As usual, Hrant most enjoyed all the singing and dancing, plus the great storytelling. So much laughter and merriment! He liked this very much.

Hrant marveled at the grace the women showed when they performed a beautifully elegant dance. Even his sisters, Nazeli and Anush joined the group. Though younger than the other women, he loved seeing how perfectly they performed the dances.

Dressed in lavishly embroidered costumes, the ladies twirled in perfect unison, leaning first to one side and then to the other, gently waving alternate hands in the air. They reminded him of fancy swans.

Then some of the men clapped their hands loudly and leaped at each other in a military-type dance, called the yarkhushta. Hrant's eyes grew wide. He looked forward to learning this dance.

When the men dashed through the crowd dancing, Hrant laughed out loud. In the air above their smiling faces, they swayed khorovats, long sticks threaded with his favorite, yummy-smelling grilled meat. Surely, he, too, would do this dance when he grew older.

Oh, yes! Food abounded. In his wildest imagination, Hrant could not envision a finer feast being possible. Enormous platters were piled high with all sorts of incredible edibles. Naturally, there were mounds of grapes and apricots, many varieties of nuts, plus figs, dates, and colorful fruits Hrant did not even recognize.

Next came trays bearing cheeses, olives, bread, and oils. He snared a peppery piece of basturma, a dried spicy beef, along with some cheese as it passed by, amidst rows of raw orange and purple carrot spears.

There were also huge baskets filled with Armenian lavash bread, of course. In fact, at one point they placed lavash on the shoulders of the bride and groom. This seemed most peculiar to Hrant, but Anush explained to him that this tradition was a sign of prosperity and abundance.

Amidst the many appetizers, he thought he must have eaten 5 or 6 mante dumplings himself. He adored drizzling yogurt on the crunchy little, boat-shaped tidbits filled with minced lamb. They all went down so easily. Yummy!

"Thank goodness," Hrant thought. A pause in the feasting occurred each time a round of happy toasts took place with various people offering good wishes for the future for the happy couple. Or there were breaks for music and dancing. For Hrant, the breaks afforded him time to walk off or dance off some of the foods he had been devouring. He did not believe he had ever eaten as much food in one day in his entire life.

The food seemed to have no end. So many delicious-looking items filled the trays, but he knew he could not possibly eat every type.

Colorful stuffed peppers, Armenian tabbouleh salad, baked eggplant, and rice pilaf all appealed to him. And he scooped up a little of his favorite tangy and spicy Armenian eech, cooked bulgur with tomato paste, vegetables, paprika, and parsley that was being served cool at this wedding feast.

As usual, Hrant especially relished smelling the various meats that had been roasting before their arrival. These had always been favorites of his for as long as he could remember. Of course, the khorovats grilled meat called to him. With his tiny hand, he deftly selected a big chunk with a burly bone.

He also gobbled up what he was certain was more than his fair share of the small, delectable Armenian shish kebab chunks, too. Hrant savored each and every delectably juicy bite.

Finally, he decided that he simply must stop. He felt as though his stomach might burst!

Of course, more music and lots more laughter abounded. Hrant remembered thinking that he had never seen nor heard as much happiness in any one place. So many toasts to the bride and groom were offered that he lost count.

By the time the chocolates and desserts came out, he felt so tired... and so full. But the sweet, honeyed pastry was too good to pass up.

Hrant bid his mother "goodnight" and selected a couple of choice pieces of pakhlava, before slipping quietly up to the rooftop to sleep. He felt such peace just lying there listening to the party continuing all around him below in the yard. Part of him longed to continue along with the revelry. But the little lad was simply too tired. Ah, such wonderful times. Such fondly cherished memories. Such a delightful reminder that, indeed, time is dear.

Even years later, Hrant could recall that special day and evening at any time. It did not matter where he was or what was going on around him. He would remember those festivities and feel himself drifting away on lovely thoughts. Unfortunately, such happy memories would linger only in his youthful past.

That special event had happened many years ago when Hrant was still a young boy. He knew that no summer adventures by the lake awaited him this year. His parents told him that the countryside had become a dangerous place. That seemed terribly sad to be happening to such a beautiful area.

In the evenings, he had heard Papa and his friends share the latest news. It was far from good.

Turkish soldiers, mountain tribesmen, newly released prisoners, and Kurdish warlords, all paid by the Young Turks, were now attacking Armenians. Those tending the vineyards had fled if they'd been able. Many sought refuge within the walls of Van itself.

Regardless, Hrant's experiences at Lake Van and within the city taught him the importance of loving and cherishing family and good friends. He learned the value of community spirit and strong faith in God. His many lessons regarding the power of these ties, as well as their life and death importance, awaited him... just around the corner.

Sweet Siblings

9

HAVING BEEN JUST three years old when Ohanes left for America, Hrant did not have a clear memory of him. Most of what he knew was learned from hearing his parents read aloud his eldest brother's letters.

But now that the second son, Aram, was also in the United States, Hrant found himself missing Aram. He had always enjoyed Aram's drawings and paintings. He especially treasured one of the artworks that Aram created and gave to Hrant.

Aram made this one all in shades of black and gray, done with charcoals. The scene was their back courtyard, and every detail was perfect. Hrant smiled each time he looked at the piece that was hanging on the wall where he slept. It helped him not miss Aram as much.

Though the third son, Vahram, was eight years older than Hrant, he often seemed the same age. He was sweet and pleasant, but his body always appeared small and weak in various ways. He stood only one inch taller than little Hrant, though he was much older.

His skin constantly appeared to be very pale. Vahram seemed thoroughly exhausted, even though he was not physically active, and he sometimes suffered great chest pains. Their mother merely explained that

Vahram was born with a rare blood disorder that caused him some difficulty breathing. None of the other children suffered this, not even his twin sister, Nazeli.

Nothing seemed to help. Hrant would hear Vahram wheezing, even when his brother was not sleeping.

Sadly, this all meant that Vahram never learned to sing or dance, but the small-framed lad could play the violin beautifully. He also played the oud, a sort of short-necked, stringed lute.

While Hrant and Vahram, studied math, languages, woodworking, and religion, all the children were also talented musicians and highly skilled in the arts of tailoring. His sisters, Nazeli and Anush, also were becoming even more skillful in their kitchen crafts, thanks to Aghavni's excellent cooking.

But tailoring was the family's primary work. Though just young teens, both sisters had gained wonderful reputations for their artistic detail in embroidering unique, colorful designs on shirt collars. And their velvet inlays on the men's suit lapels and collars were always perfectly straight.

Hrant remembered relishing seeing their work in the fancy garments worn by guests at that big wedding on the island. Yet, Hrant realized, that their tailoring skills did not stop there.

As deftly as Nazeli and Anush embroidered, they wove fine Armenian lace, too. Plus, they stitched everything from uniforms to daily alterations.

Hrant was accustomed to seeing them working from dawn to sundown. Because Ottoman law did not permit women to work, they only did so in the privacy of the Gulumian home, never going to the tailor shop.

They also studied secretly. Though they had attended Armenian elementary schools, they now continued their education at home, where the teachers regularly visited. They learned from books that the boys brought home. Both girls could read and write very well.

Over the years, they had received some special books as gifts from their Papa when he returned from his travels as a merchant. A couple of these books had come from America, as well as from Europe.

However, these they hid down below the house in the vegetable cellar. No one wanted to risk having the Ottomans discover that these Armenians were teaching their girls to read, never mind speak, understand, and read *foreign* languages. Papa always reminded them of the old proverb's teaching that it is sometimes better to be learned, but be taken for ignorant.

This all seemed rather unfair to Hrant. If the Armenians recognized that girls could and should study and learn, why didn't everyone else? He did not understand why the Ottomans did not want women to be educated beyond home skills and social customs.

Strong and outspoken, Mother was actively involved in the Union of Armenian Women of the Caucasus. She had organized the entire family's participation for years, even before Hrant was born.

Aghavni also made certain that the sisters helped in the gathering of clothing and supplies for widows and orphans, and more recently, Armenian refugees. They had been arriving in the walled city in growing numbers due to all the area villages and towns being increasingly sacked by the Ottoman military forces.

Both Nazeli and Anush worked hard, but Hrant loved watching Anush best. Nazeli was always kind and good to him. She was beautiful. And she was gentle and soft-spoken, like Papa and Aram.

But the younger Anush joked and chuckled. When she caught him watching her, Anush made funny faces to make him giggle, too.

The younger of the two sisters was an olive-skinned, spirited beauty with laughing almond-shaped dark gray eyes and a vivaciously sparkling personality. Mother quietly talked to her every morning as she combed through her long, wavy dark hair. This was their special time for calming, learning, and advice sharing. Anush was young, and their parents feared she was too high-spirited.

Hrant thought that trying to tame Anush was akin to taming a wild horse. He liked her spirit and humor very much. Plus, she was very talented and showed great artistry in her work.

Anush's skillful hands in sewing were only matched by her good sense in the kitchen. Hrant was not sure which he liked more. Was it watching his sister prepare the aromatic herbs and spices for the shish kebab or sitting spellbound at her feet, listening to her weave fantastic stories that made his eyes grow wide with wonder? Whatever she was doing, his favorite sister always made him laugh.

Both of his sisters also spent time in the evening making lace and delicate appliques for Nazeli's wedding dress. The elder sister was engaged to marry Toros Kherbekian, the son of a highly successful merchant who'd been a friend of their family for many years. The entire family was pleased with the planned union that would now take place just as soon as Toros returned from military service.

Hrant liked Toros very much. He was handsome, witty, and musical. He also taught Hrant some fancy new dance steps he had learned while away at the university.

Toros was most marvelous and fashionable by anyone's definition. The youngest Gulumian child found himself openly glad that Toros would soon be his new brother.

So, Hrant missed him, too. Sadly, Toros had been in an early wave of young Armenian men ordered into the military by the edict from the Young Turks.

Then came the rumors that the Armenians' weapons had been confiscated, and the men were sent to work in manual labor camps building the Ottoman Empire's railroad. Later, they learned that this news was no longer a mere rumor.

However, the Gulumians, as with all Armenians, were not about to give up hope. They kept their beloved Toros in their prayers. They always spoke of the glorious day when he would return from the front, and the Gulumians would again host a beautiful wedding, this time for Nazeli and Toros.

Unfortunately, the incoming news did not seem supportive of any gleeful family celebrations on any close horizon. Grave peril festered, far too close to home.

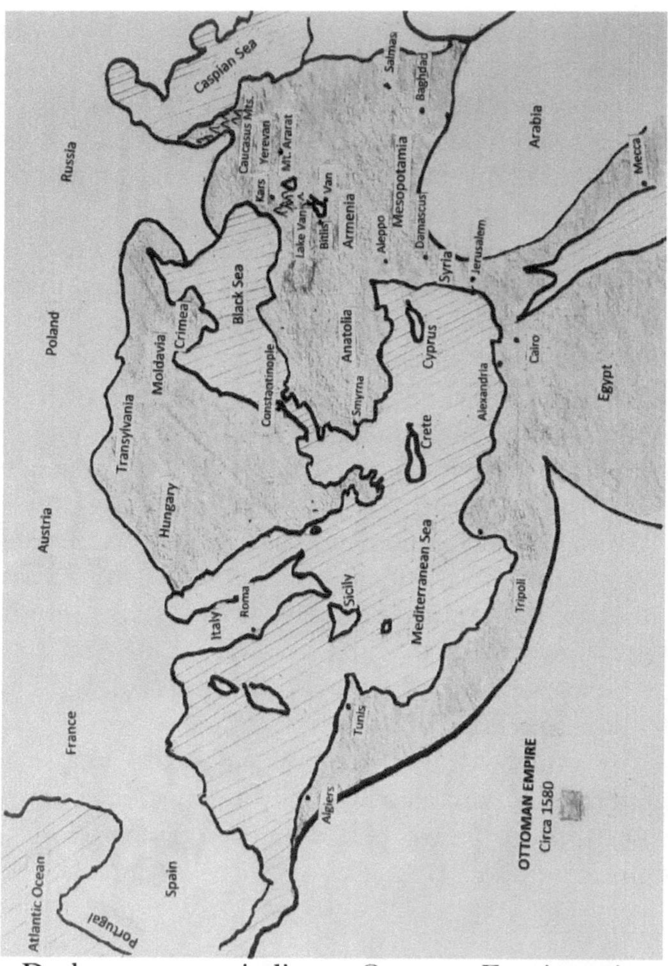

Darker gray area indicates Ottoman Empire at its height, circa 1580, showing clear domination throughout Mediterranean and Black Sea regions

The Younger Ohanes
10

THE ELDEST GULUMIAN son, Ohanes, Ohan for short, had been sent to America a few years after the Ottoman slaughter of Armenians that had occurred from 1894 - 1896. The Hamidian massacres started when Ohan was just 6 years old. The family decided that Armenia was no place for him to build a life. So, they completed the plans for him to emigrate, which he did, setting sail on the Oceania toward New York City the day after his 21st birthday.

Ohan worked hard. By day, he had secured a steady job at the Victoria Shoe factory in East Boston. He settled there and found private tailoring work to do on the side in the evenings. By 1915, he was proudly well into the process of becoming a United States citizen.

Ohanes, or John, as he was called in the States, also worked diligently to get information to and from his family back in Armenia. He had befriended several individuals who helped him become active in the Armenian resistance movement from afar.

Boston's Dr. Paul Corasian was among those raising money to help refugees and fellow countrymen. So many people were attempting to flee from Armenia and come to America or go to other places that were safe from the Ottomans.

"You have all done very well helping displaced Armenians reconnect with loved ones, from whom they had become separated during the escape attempts and forced marches." Dr. Corasian always thanked his volunteers, including John and now his brother, Aram.

"The Ottomans here in the Boston consulate office have tried but failed to break our information-sharing network. Our success continues through several nations. However, the news of late inspires great concern."

As he detailed tragic news, alarm bells sounded in John's mind, but he felt utterly powerless to help his family. However, like Dr. Corasian, he knew his father and grandfather were well connected with the Armenian resistance. They would be both prepared to fight and have an escape plan for the family, as well.

John spoke up. "Dr. Corasian, my family in Van all hoped and prayed that this time of trouble with the Ottomans, would pass, and life could return to a sort of calm. The new Young Turk leadership talked of tolerance of the Christians and respect for the Armenian nation's existence there for thousands of years."

"Oh, yes, Ohan," the doctor responded. "Many Armenians had expressed relief and gratitude. However, many *more* remained highly skeptical. Sadly, the skeptics are now being proven to be correct. Aram Manukian was right. There will be no calm. No unity. No peace."

John had tried to accept that these difficulties were simply their cross to bear for being Christians in a Muslim world... and for being Armenians, of course. Still, he often found news of the atrocities most challenging to simply accept.

"Doctor, why do the Ottomans not understand that they are behaving as savages and backward-thinking people? Pardon me for being outspoken, but they are the opposite of progressive or modern in their thinking." John continued, "There is no tolerance. There is no mercy!"

"You are starting to understand the gravity of the situation," replied Dr. Corasian. "Their once vast Ottoman Empire is crumbling. What sufficed in past decades and centuries will no longer be tolerated as people gain education. Their failure could not possibly be their own fault. Of course not! They relish blaming their failures, ignorance, and issues on somebody else. That somebody is the Armenians.

"We must be punished and removed from all provinces, including our six Armenian provinces. Adding insult to injury, the leaders then replace Armenians with Turkish families. Remember, if a nation's leaders are hell-bent on savagery, any excuse will serve their purposes.

Aram now spoke up. "Repeatedly, Armenian leaders have been promised that if their cities surrendered to the Ottoman military, the residents would be spared. Instead, the massacres started as soon as the army entered. Blessedly, some people managed to flee into the mountains. It seems unthinkable that even churches and cemeteries are proving to be unsuitable for safe refuge."

John was surprised to hear such passion coming from Aram. His brother had typically been a man of very few words. Well, that was before he had started teaching in Armenia.

Dr. Corasian replied. "Do not expect the Ottomans to show respect for God or His children. Their behavior is ungodly, most assuredly. They have made their hatred for us quite clear. Still, their horrific acts have proven to be purely anti-human, not just anti-Christian. To say they are un-Godlike would be far too kind and generous."

Everyone in the room agreed. News accountings told the previously unimaginable truth. Many Armenians, both young and old, were slaughtered on the streets and in churches. Survivors were being rounded up and exiled toward the Syrian deserts and Mesopotamia.

Photographs and eyewitness accounts arrived in Boston and throughout the world. They showed long columns of Armenians being forced by military guards to walk for days, often with no food nor water. In many cases, the refugees had been stripped of all their clothing and belongings. Their bodies blistered from exposure. Reports grew in frequency regarding countless attacks by bandits and of the women being sexually abused by both thugs and guards.

Tens of thousands of Armenians were dying from injuries, illness, and exposure along the torturous walks. Adding insult to injury, Armenians were forced to unceremoniously abandon the bodies of loved ones along roadsides.

Worse yet, if the situation could be any worse, the people from many villages were simply forced out of their homes and marched out of their towns, only to be executed along the supposed evacuation routes. Others were put in prisons where they were tortured daily. Many Armenians were tortured on the main streets of their own villages with powerless friends and family members compelled to watch.

Dr. Corasian spoke again. "The Ottoman leaders continue to contend that they are merely relocating a minority population for *our* safety. The Young Turks are doing this for *our* own good. Do they think anyone other than their own subjects would ever possibly believe such maligned drivel? It matters not how many times they repeat it, nor how loudly they protest to the civilized worlds' admonishments. They would not know a humanitarian act if their lives depended on it."

"Oh, wait," John said. "I forgot. Our people are *not* being exiled. What was I thinking? Pardon my confusion. Armenians are merely being relocated to areas that are *safer* for *us*." Even in his sarcasm, he could not get over the idiocy reflected in the Young Turks' explanation for what was taking place in his homeland.

Dr. Corasian gently lifted one hand. His understanding was clear as he spoke. "This is why we work tirelessly. Removing us or killing us off is the only way the Ottomans can take away our majority in the six Armenian provinces. They are barbaric. We must not stoop to their level."

John had long ago lost all comprehension of how the Turks could be so grossly intolerant and filled with such hatred. The Armenians had been a peace-loving people for countless generations. They worked hard. They managed to prosper despite the extra taxes heaped on them by their Turkish rulers.

Ah, there's the "rub." The Armenians persisted.

With Aram at his side, John enjoyed time with his mentor. Dr. Paul Corasian had become a friend and true father figure. He had also served as a witness on John's application to be considered for United States citizenship. John trusted him.

Dr. Corasian tried to add perspective. Aram and John always listened intently to the kindly gentleman.

"Aram. Ohan. New Turkish leadership and hopeful words changed nothing," the good doctor began. "There will be no unity. Remember that the wolf changes its skin, but not its nature.

"Our peace, our prosperity, and our faith cause great jealousy, even in the Young Turks. They want what we have. They want our businesses, our homes, our education, and they want our talents and skills. They simply do not wish to work to earn any of it. They prefer to take what they want... or destroy it. They believe that forcing people to live in total dependence on them somehow makes them leaders.

"We know far better. What the Ottoman Turks fail to understand is that they can drive us from our homes, banish us from our lands, and even slaughter countless of our brethren. However, they cannot destroy Armenia. It lives on always. It lives within our souls. Never forget that."

The young Armenian men understood the good doctor. They had seen it in their Turkish friends. While John and Aram grew up, working hard every day, they also studied hard and learned to honor their family, church, and culture.

Most of the Ottoman Turkish boys they had grown up with did not even go to school. They had not been keen on learning trades. They had shown no interest in art nor music. At the time, it had simply not seemed to be an important part of their culture.

The good doctor calmly continued. "As has been customary for a long time, Turkish boys tend to grow up and enter the military, unless they have connections with ranking members of the government. Then, of course, they join the swelling numbers of people working in government capacities. For goods and services, they turn to the Armenians."

"Then why," queried John, "do so many Turks speak in anger that the Armenians own all the ships and shops, livestock and crops, and run numerous publishing concerns and educational facilities? Part of our Armenian culture includes working hard to help every member of our families reach their full potential."

"Yes, Ohan," interjected Aram. "And that includes the women."

"You are right again," said the doctor. "Turkish rules still do not allow the population counts to even include females. They do not permit women's names to be listed in record books. As you well know, women cannot work nor leave their neighborhoods. They must wear veils over their faces when leaving the Armenian quarter, and always be escorted by a man."

John had known several women who were noteworthy scholars, but rules necessitated them writing under male names. If they could not attend a foreign university, they completed all the same studies in the privacy of their homes. All such things as this were done in great secrecy, for penalties could be most severe. It was as though the Ottomans felt sadly threatened by women's strength and promise.

He already had gratefully observed that while things were not perfect, they were certainly far better for women in the United States. They could not yet vote in elections, but that appeared to be very close to changing. Yes, life for women and everyone else seemed to offer far more potential in America than anywhere else.

What John likely did not realize was that the contacts and friends he had made in Boston would play a major role in his family's story. The future generations, including Cassie's, would be stunned.

Boston, Massachusetts
Courtesy of Boston Public Library

The Great War
11

RUMORS OF WAR between England and Germany escalated in the Spring of 1914. Whisperings hinted more strongly that the Ottomans planned to start or at least engage in a war. Representing the Young Turks, the Three Pashas then signed the Secret Ottoman-German Alliance in August.

This officially pitted Turkey against Russia and England, two of many nations supportive of the Armenians. Thus, by Fall, the Armenian situation in the Ottoman Empire took a sharp, downward turn.

The Turks abruptly started closing Armenian schools wherever they wished to use them as military barracks. Many Armenian families turned their homes into classrooms. Interestingly, this twist of Fate provided the first advanced classroom experience for Armenian girls in many decades.

Ismail Enver Pasha, the Minister of War, began signing many orders against the Ottoman Empire's Armenian citizens. He demanded all able-bodied Armenian men join the Turkish army, effectively clearing fit men from all towns and cities in the six Armenian provinces. This came in preparation for the "deportation" endeavors.

For many years, the Ottoman leadership had made it clear that it did not want to arm its heathen Armenians. Recently, however, someone had proposed a very dark, but creative way to handle the challenge. They could order the Armenian young men to bring their own weapons, which would then be confiscated, naturally. Then they would force Armenians into labor camps to clear roads and build the Young Turks' railroad. Or, of course, Ottoman commanders could then simply march the Armenians out into fields and shoot them all.

The Gulumians felt fortunate. So many of the tailors were old enough that the government had not wanted them to answer the military call. Being over age forty, Garabed and his father ranked in the group considered to be "too old."

Vahram, though of proper age, was bypassed as he was deemed not able-bodied, due to his extremely small size and his rare blood disorder's other effects. Unfortunately, Nazeli's betrothed, Toros, had been forced to join the Ottoman army.

Another order commanded the remaining male elders and Armenian women to turn in all weapons to the local authorities. The few weapons confiscated from the women were served up as proof to Constantinople that local forces had indeed stopped an Armenian revolutionary uprising. Seriously.

Enver Pasha, officially the Supreme Commander of the Ottoman armed forces, also decreed all Armenians were "traitors against the Turkish government." This was based purely on their ongoing, positive relationship with England.

On the streets, Armenians stopped wearing the colors red, white, and blue together, as the Turks felt that showed Armenians favored the Ottoman Empire's war enemies. The Pasha even issued orders for the capture of many Armenians, dead or alive.

Then came Christmas, but Armenians found little to celebrate. Everyone doubted that the usual lavish feasts in the town square would even be considered this winter. Families struggled due to the existence of primarily just the women, children, and elderly left in the homes and businesses. Many businesses closed altogether, for the women were not permitted by the Turks to help run them, at least not officially or publicly, even under these extreme circumstances.

"We must all pray," began Garabed to his family one December evening, fast approaching Christmas. "We must pray for the success of the European allies as war is waged against the Central Powers. Indeed, a great war has begun. This war is most important. Without military defeat, the Ottoman Empire will be left to continue its trek down a very dangerously destructive and intolerant path."

"Papa?" Looking at his father, Hrant batted the long eyelashes framing his sparkling, deep hazel eyes, and he finished chewing his last bite of a juicy slice of his mother's famous pakhlava before continuing.

"Yes, son. What is it?" Garabed replied with a scant smile at his son's earnest query, delivered with seriously scrunched eyebrows.

The little lad posed his question. "What if we all pray for peace instead of war?"

Garabed's reply came without hesitation. "Believe me, son. We want nothing more than peace. Sadly, some people are power-hungry. They seem to thrive on battling against other people. If other people... or I should say, if *we* do not at least *try* to stand up to them at some point, it could be too late. All could be lost. You can be sure that we only fight when there is absolutely no other course of action. We only fight in self-defense."

"I think that is good," said Hrant. "So many of us feel sad right now. But I remember the priest saying that Jesus was the Prince of Peace."

"Yes, Hrant, you are right." His father continued. "And His name shall be called Wonderful. So, when we pray for peace, we are asking for peace even if we must pass through highly troubled waters to get there."

Hrant looked to the side a bit as he paused. He formulated an idea.

"Mama, may I go upstairs and out on the balcony?" His voice sounded eager.

"Of course, you can," Aghavni replied. "Please put on your jacket and scarf first. It is very cold outside."

Without another word, Hrant scrambled to his feet and scurried up the stairs. Garabed, Aghavni, the elder Ohanes, Nazeli, Vahram, and Anush all looked back and forth at each other. They shrugged. No one seemed to have a clue as to what was in the youngest Gulumian child's mind.

"Hark! The herald angels sing, Glory to the newborn King! Peace on earth and mercy mild, God and sinners reconciled.'"

They had not had long to wait. Hrant's sweet, clear voice rang out through the night air from the balcony above them. He was singing Christmas carols for all the neighborhood to hear.

Within a moment, everyone else had scrambled to their feet. Quickly donning jackets, hats, and shawls, they stepped out the front door and looked up at

Hrant, singing his little heart out from the balcony above.

One by one, neighbors began opening their doors and stepping out to see Hrant's performance. Garabed immediately joined his son by singing along. The rest of the family joined also. By the time Hrant began the second carol, half the neighborhood seemed to be united in song.

"Joy to the world! The Lord is come. Let earth receive her King. Let every heart prepare Him room. And heaven and nature sing. And heaven and nature sing. And heaven, and heaven and nature sing."

On the outside, the world did not seem to be a particularly joy-filled place. But for this moment in time, the youngest son managed to stir hearts in his own family and inspire the neighbors to set aside fears and handwringing, at least for this one evening. Perhaps their joy could last through the Christmas season.

They needed to savor these cherished moments. Sadly, whatever measure of joy they felt would be short-lived.

Photo courtesy of Hans Braxmeier

Letters and Learning
12

CASSIE'S GRANDMOTHER HAD written down her memoirs in her elder years as a sort of journal for her grandchildren. Cassie herself would later publish them as a memoir, *Of the Same Blood: Your Eurasian Heritage.* Her grandmother's words spoke about Grampa Hrant's story.

As Marjorie Rowe Gulumian wrote:

> "His oldest brother, Ohanes, was working in the United States as the personal tailor for a highly extolled, successful man, an alleged bootlegger named Kennedy in Massachusetts. (Yes, the same one who spawned the political dynasty.) Kennedy's reportedly bootleg money got my father to this country, but it wasn't easy."

Some of the struggles, referenced by Marjorie, are reflected in the family letters. Most letters the family received from the United States were read and shared, only to be burned afterward, so they could not fall into the wrong hands. A precious few remained.

The weekly mail delivery always included a letter from Boston, including this one received in March 1915.

Dear Mother and Father,

I am pleased to tell you that I just put the finishing details on a new suit for Mr. Kennedy. It is ready just in time for a celebration in East Boston at his third establishment. This is near where I am now living.

My daily job is going very well at the Victoria Shoe Factory, and I am saving money. We will buy a farm for the family. We can start over here away from the suffering. If you insist, you can go home later, when troubles cease.

New arrivals from Armenia echo the published reports. The attacks are getting much closer to you. They will never let our precious Van stand.

I have good contact now with our ambassador and have saved money for your passage. We must get you all out as soon as possible.

I can also cover passage for Toros, Nazeli's betrothed. Perhaps the marriage will be best to take place here in Boston.

Further, I have met Kudrat Bogijian, a nephew of a highly respected carpet merchant here in Boston. I have confidence that Papa and Grandfather will agree that Kudrat will make a pleasant and most suitable husband for young Anush. You will all meet the family when you arrive in America.

I have filed my formal application for United States citizenship. In doing so, I had to denounce the Sultan.

As father always says, "Time is dear." I say to you that the time for your travel is now.

With my love and deepest respect,

Ohanes

In April, Aghavni wrote to John. In finding these treasured remembrances of family members, Grandmother Marjorie could not determine whether Aghavni had yet received Ohan's previous letter when writing this one to her son.

Dearest Ohanes,

I pray this letter reaches you, and that you know how proud we are of you and the hard work you are doing. Please remember how much we all love you. Plans are made, but we hope to not need them. As you know, all we want is peace and unity.

We are saddened to report that Toros, Nazeli's betrothed, was forced into military service by the Ottomans. Unfortunately, we have learned he cannot be located with the unit to which he was sent. Nazeli fears the worst. We are trying to keep her spirits up, and we are utilizing all avenues to gain information.

We have heard that many of these young men have been imprisoned or killed. Sometimes they have been sent to the front lines, often without weapons. This is beyond unthinkable.

We are Armenians. We have suffered much. God help us to survive this.

You have probably already read in the newspapers about all the growing troubles in Constantinople. We lost beloved friends and leaders.

Despite the warnings, Papa and your grandfather remain active with the resistance here in Van and in helping refugees throughout the provinces. There are so many suffering Armenians in need of our assistance.

We are praying for the best, but we are also preparing for the very worst. Wringing our hands and worrying will do us no good, but the fear of the wolf will not make us forget our village.

So many survivors from the neighboring villages are here already.

We provide refuge within our quarters, but crowding is becoming an issue. We cannot believe the Turks would destroy Van as they have other cities. Van has been central in our history for thousands of years.

With God's grace, we will be together again.

All our love to you,

Mother

Marjorie Rowe Gulumian admitted she had fallen in love and married into the Armenian family with total ignorance of their culture, never mind their struggles. A typical American, she had much to learn.

The eldest child and only daughter in an Irish family, Marjorie's father and five uncles had all gone to Dartmouth College and medical school. Marjorie felt blessed to also be able to receive higher education, and she hoped to become a teacher one day. She loved people and reading and chose psychology as her major at the University of New Hampshire in Durham.

Here is more of what she wrote years later in her journal about Armenia. She openly admitted having everything to discover and understand.

"So, I looked into Armenia and learned. As a child, I had no friends who had even heard of Armenia. As adults, most of us knew pitifully little.

"Armenia is legendary and considered hallowed ground by most scholars. Lush with high mountains, rivers such as the Tigris and Euphrates begin there. Mount Ararat is where Noah's ark is said to have come to rest. It is also believed that Armenia was home to the Garden of Eden. Armenia was one of the very first nations to accept Christianity.

"There was widespread regional perception and acceptance of the cultural and intellectual superiority of the Armenians. At that time, Armenian women were not permitted to work outside the home. However, they were the leaders in the home and lorded over all manner of raising and educating the children and running the households. When the Turks and Huns could no longer stand the existence of the "superior race," decisions were made to eliminate them.

"The destruction of a civilized society by a jealous, violent one is never a good thing for anyone involved."

At the time she wrote her journals, Marjorie Gulumian lacked full details about her husband's personal journey and traumas, but she knew what he had shared with Cassie and her. She had since researched and learned a great deal more. Sadness unabashedly flowed as she recognized how close she came to never being able to meet her beloved husband, Hrant. Her journal continues.

"I have learned that what your grandfather saw in the once beautiful streets of Van has mountains of historic evidence. These facts cannot be erased, despite constantly repeated denials by the Turks. Denials that continue for decades!

"Indeed, there was a concentrated, government-organized endeavor to eliminate all the boys throughout Van to prevent the possibility of them growing up and retaliating against the Turks. I am being judicious in choosing those words. In truth, there was an official order given to kill every Armenian male in Van. Some Turkish historians have tried to justify this fact by stating that it was most likely a response to what they called an "Armenian revolution" centered in Van.

"I found that interesting. Because I'd heard the story from someone who had lived it, I knew more. I knew better. Grampa's Dad had done what other brave souls had done in Van. After learning of increasing massacres of Armenians in other regions, they knew they could sit and wait for the barbarians to be at their doors, or they could try to push them back. They formed a resistance movement to protect their homes and their city. They had few guns because the Turks had confiscated weapons. However, everyone worked to make ammunition. Or prepare marksmen. Or dig trenches for the Armenian defenses. My husband's father and grandfather were indeed among the resistance leaders."

Writing her journal caused Marjorie to stop and ponder what life must have been like for Hrant when he was just a small boy in those times of great uncertainty, lies, misinformation, and turmoil. She knew his experiences and family foundation taught him to open his eyes, instead of opening his mouth.

A Secret Discovery
13

KNOWING THAT HIS brothers, parents, and grandfather were helping Armenians who were in deep trouble brought some comfort to Hrant. This became especially important during the times his Papa was away from home.

Hrant had grown accustomed to his Papa and Grampa coming home for dinner every night. Now, with increasing frequency, the men would be away for several days at a time.

When they were home, there was more whispering, more evenings when various friends gathered for late-night, private conversations in the walled courtyard. Hrant missed the colorful evenings of merriment and music.

On one occasion, Garabed and his father, the senior Ohanes, had been absent from the home for three days. Hrant wasn't the only one getting antsy. His sisters continued to sew and work on their chores, but he heard noticeably less giggling and chit-chatting between them.

His mother, Aghavni, remained steadfast. Regardless of what was going on, she somehow managed to appear calm and unshakable. That made Hrant feel reassured that everything would somehow turn out fine.

As usual, Mama was busily preparing food, not yet knowing whether her husband and father-in-law would get back home on this day or some other day. Vahram was napping, as he often did to regain some strength in his overly slight teenaged frame. Nazeli and Anush were upstairs finishing some clothing items that needed to go back to the tailor shop in the morning.

Just because the men were away, the work did not stop. They had a small team that ran the shop seamlessly in their absence. The ladies maintained their work vigilantly at home, often working long hours into the night. This afternoon looked like it would turn into one of those nights.

Hrant's classic patience had not yet evolved. The lad had grown weary sitting on the little kitchen stool watching Mama. He casually meandered into the back courtyard to continue whittling his new flute.

Upon hearing one of the horses snorting in its stall, he turned and entered the small stable, which was attached to the house on one side of the courtyard. This was not a fancy horse barn, as one might see in America, but it protected their horses. There were three stalls along the wall that backed onto the courtyard, and about an eight-foot-wide open area along the outside wall. That space was stacked with bales of hay, plus a barrel of grain. Hooks and shelves on the wall held spare bridles, bits, blankets, and other supplies.

Only one saddle hung on the wall since both Garabed and the senior Ohanes were out on their horses. Only one horse, named Asbed, remained.

The late afternoon sun glowed through one of the small windows, spinning Asbed's coat into shiny gold. Hrant smiled. He reached up and petted her velvety soft snout. She was a gentle favorite of his.

Glancing to the side, Hrant spied something he had not previously seen. Could it be?

He stepped closer. He knew the way to the vegetable cellar, but this was altogether new to him. He crouched down and looked more intently.

Sure enough, he had found the corner of a trap door in the floor! Pushing the usual bales of hay to the side, he could see heavy hinges and a latch. He tugged with all his might, but the door only lifted a few inches. It proved to be too heavy for him to lift all the way up.

Thankfully, Hrant had good reasoning skills, even as a young lad. He quickly found that if he lifted one corner just a little, he could wedge something under it and keep it open that sliver amount. He then grabbed a nearby board for some leverage.

Slipping one end under the raised corner of the door, Hrant then leaned all his weight on the other end. Sure enough, the trap door rose more. He then used his foot to push a bale of hay under the widest opening. Hrant released the board and scurried to push another bale under the opposite corner.

He laid on his stomach and eased his tiny frame through the opening to peer inside. Spying the rungs of what appeared to be a sort of ladder, he slowly lowered himself into the unknown cavern below.

Hrant could tell he was standing on a dirt floor. He blinked his eyes a few times, letting the cool darkness envelop him. *What is this place? Why* had he not known of its existence? *How* had he not known?

He reached out one hand, slowly extending his arm until his fingers touched dirt walls. As his eyes began to adjust a little to the darkness, it appeared to Hrant that space seemed to vanish into an inky blackness in two directions.

Wow! What a discovery this lad had made! Just wait until he showed his friends *this!* Of course, they would need candles or a lantern to go exploring.

"Hrant! Hrant Gulumian! Where are you?!?" Aghavni's nervous voice split the silent darkness.

Without delay, he scurried up the make-shift ladder. Pressing his torso between his carefully placed bales of hay propping open the trap door, Hrant felt two strong hands grab him by the shoulders and pull him harshly to his feet. Only then did he see the wide-eyed terror in his dear mother's face.

"No! No! No! No! No! No!" Mama kept repeating, sternly shaking her head for emphasis.

As he got to his feet, Hrant brushed off his clothes. His mother moved the bales of hay and closed the trap door. She then carefully placed the bales back over the door, disguising its existence completely.

He stood perfectly still as his mother hurriedly worked. The bales were in their original places, and she even scattered a bit of loose hay about on the floor around them. When she was done, it appeared as though no trap door ever existed.

"This is *not* for play!" Mama's voice sounded deadly serious. He knew his curiosity had gotten him into miserably hot water.

She continued. "This is not something we talk about, not now, not ever!"

Aghavni placed her hands on his shoulders and looked him directly in his eyes. Her voice softened. "Promise me, Hrant. Promise me you will not go down there again, and you will speak of it to no one."

"I promise, Mama," Hrant sincerely said without hesitation. He did not understand what it was, but he knew not to cross his mother. She was kind to him always, but serious. And she was utterly serious now.

After he spoke, her face softened. The fear left her eyes. She then slowly closed her eyes and paused a moment, before opening them and speaking again.

"I will have your father explain the tunnel when he returns. We will not speak of it again until then. Come, son. You need to eat now."

Well, there it was. A tunnel! The elephant in the room that no one was to mention! This dark mystery would now constantly loom in Hrant's mind, even after his father took him into the tunnel and explained it was for an emergency only.

Hrant could not fathom what sort of emergency could make a tunnel so important. Yet, he trusted his family, and especially his parents.

Little did Hrant or any of them realize how very soon that trap door might open again. Nor did they know if it would or would not be for their escape.

Photo courtesy of Peter Lutz

Parental Wisdom

14

GARABED'S RETURN ALWAYS brought a bustle of activity with it. Men from the market district arrived with large bundles of clothing, shoes, food, and other goods. Armenians worked hard for everything they earned. They also shared most generously every time people hit hard times. These certainly constituted the hardest of times.

Small sacks brimmed with a variety of nuts and dried fruits. There were also crates with bread and fried lamb. These were foods that traveled well and lasted for some length of time. These items would help feed growing numbers of refugees and displaced Armenians both within the walled city and throughout their province.

Enormous piles of clothing included shoes, jackets, pants, shirts, skirts, vests, and more. Hrant thought it very impressive how generous people were. He knew that many of the people donating items did not have all that much themselves. However, an awareness prevailed that some had less and suffered greater need.

He spied a nice variety of donated books. Hrant recalled his mother scolding him when he had once thoughtlessly snatched up a book in a delivery the men were unloading. She then reminded him that he already owned many books. These items were for families that had lost everything. He had set the book down immediately, but he looked at it longingly.

Aghavni suggested a way he might have that book. He eagerly awaited details.

"All right, son." Mama continued. "You may keep that book. However, you must first donate three of your books in its place."

"Why not just one of my books for one book?" Hrant's question was sincere. A one-for-one exchange sounded fair.

His mother had taken young Hrant aside. They sat in a couple of chairs facing each other.

"Son," she began. "Try to imagine what it must be like to be kicked out of your own home. To have everything you own set on fire. You would have no clothing, except what you were wearing. You would have no books, no musical instruments, no art. All our food would be gone. There would be no furniture, not as much as a single blanket for our entire family. Do you understand how blessed we are?"

Hrant nodded sheepishly. Now he felt sad.

"No, dearest, do not feel dismayed." Aghavni sighed before continuing. "We are fortunate to not need charity. We help other people, not as fortunate as we are. They have also worked very hard, just as we do. Through no fault of their own, Armenians are losing their homes. They are losing everything they have. They are losing family members. We simply do what we can to help with daily needs. Do you understand?"

"Yes, Mama," Hrant replied. He truly did grasp the suffering. People were eagerly sharing their food rations. Their clothing. Their personal possessions.

Hrant stood up and went to his room. When he returned, he held six books in his hands. He took them to the piles the men were still unloading and added them atop the other books. He turned and saw his mother watching him.

"Do you not want that particular book that arrived?" She smiled at him, nodding, letting him know it was all right.

"No, Mama," the young lad began. "I thought about it. I still have a couple of books I have not yet started reading anyway. These books that I donate I have read several times. Perhaps someone else needs them more than I do now."

Aghavni drew Hrant close to her. She hugged him warmly. "Thank you, son. You have the heart and mind of a great man." Then his mother rejoined the women who were helping to sort the arriving goods.

Hrant would not forget that lesson taught by his mother. He knew his parents were very loving, though strict. They were intelligent and compassionate. Both had regularly taught the children important lessons to help them live better lives.

Now, several weeks later, Hrant watched his sisters, his mother, her friend Hulianna Terlemezian, and a couple of other ladies from the neighborhood separating donations by type. His sisters grouped foods. The women sorted clothing by type and item. Household goods got bundled.

Hrant joined the ladies. He could fold blankets. So, he set about doing so. Even his sisters were impressed by how neatly and perfectly he stacked his little piles.

All these goods would be immediately taken for distribution to the refugees. The people seemed to be arriving daily and in ever-increasing numbers.

Very soon, the sorting ended. Everyone carried the items to the awaiting carts outside, and they departed, gratefully pulled by the volunteers who would fulfill the local distributions.

Of course, a personal reality loomed largely. All the hustle and bustle merely delayed the inevitable. This was his Papa's first night back. Hrant knew a respite was unlikely.

Sure enough, after dinner, Hrant saw his mother take Garabed aside. The little lad knew the moment he dreaded lay straight ahead. She was telling Papa about him finding the secret tunnel. He observed concern in his father's eyes as he glanced at Hrant a couple of times. But there was no anger.

When she was done speaking quietly with him, Mama immediately turned and left the room. Papa slowly walked to a corner of the room. He sat down in a chair.

For Hrant, time stood still. It simply stopped. Completely. He stood frozen in his spot. He could barely breathe.

A few moments passed as Garabed appeared to study the floor. He then looked up and directly at Hrant. He crooked his index finger, motioning for the boy to approach his father.

Without hesitation, Hrant ran to Garabed and threw his arms around his father's neck. Garabed scooped his youngest boy up onto his lap. After hugging him, he began to softly speak.

"So, young Hrant, what did you learn today in school?" His father began the conversation with his usual opening question, though the boy knew this was not where this conversation would end.

"I did perfect work on my math lessons," Hrant dutifully replied. "And I engaged in several conversations all in French, without a single Armenian word." Hrant answered, but he trembled in doing so. Argh! Could his father not get to the real point?

The lad knew this conversation would not be going in the typical direction of other evenings. There would be no tales of the road nor speculations of what life would be like when Hrant grew up.

Papa nodded slowly before speaking again. Hrant tightened his lips, preparing for whatever came next.

"Mama told me what you found in the stable. Do you know what we must do now, Hrant?" Garabed's eyebrows raised.

Hrant's own eyes widened. He ever so slowly shook his head. Noooo. He had no idea what his father meant. What did he intend to do?

"You have just turned 9 years old. You are ready. It is time to take you into the tunnel," Garabed said matter-of-factly.

With that, his father rose, lifting Hrant and setting him on his feet. He picked up a nearby lantern and headed for the stable, with his youngest son close on his heels.

At the bottom of the ladder, Garabed pointed to the left and explained that several of their friends' homes were connected in that direction. Then he turned to the right and led Hrant north.

Very soon they emerged from the tunnel into a large, stone-lined room. In the light from the lantern, Hrant could see another tunnel opening on a side wall. His father led him in a different direction... across the floor, around a huge rock, and up some uneven steps, also made of rough stone.

They wove, turned a few corners, passed down some shorter tunnels, and, finally, emerged outside, amidst some boulders. In just a few more steps, they continued climbing along a rough trail.

The path led them high above the city onto what appeared to be an expansive stone-lined terrace of sorts. They were below the medieval Urartian fortification, on a part of the ruins of the ancient fortress that came to be called the Van Castle. This terrace had been used for large Urartian ceremonial events during ancient times, back in the Bronze and Iron Ages of Armenia.

Hrant was impressed that the peculiar stairway was so well disguised as to not have been discovered by everyone. He knew, of course, about the normal paths leading to the fortress at the top. He knew of the abundance of spring water there and the many irrigation channels their ancient ancestors had built that still delivered fresh, clean water to everyone.

However, he had not known anything of the meandering caves and tunnels in the underbelly of the city... only of a great many caves beyond the city's walls. He knew he was to never attempt to enter any of them, as they notoriously served as hide-outs for wanted criminals and other outlaws.

He recalled how much he enjoyed classes that taught the students about ancient Babylonian world maps from the 5th Century BC, clearly showing the Armenian Empire. And he liked learning how the rich volcanic soil in this region led to Armenia becoming one of the world's earliest sites of agricultural activity with a great many orchards.

Perhaps some had been early renditions of the orchards by Lake Van that he greatly enjoyed now. He had often pictured what his family would have been like back then. He presumed they would have been farmers, but also tailors, of course.

Hrant had previously visited the stone stables, where he learned oxen and sheep were kept before being sacrificed to the Urartian gods. While such practices struck him as strange, he recognized that these were ancient people, hundreds of years before Jesus was even born.

He also remembered marveling at the smooth rock floors and being shown the royal chambers. The meanings of the many inscriptions on the walls remained a mystery to him.

Garabed took Hrant's hand and led him toward an edge overlooking the city. They sat down. From his studies, Hrant recalled that the rock terrace on this southeastern slope had been a sacred place for rituals. It measured 40 by 15 meters.

Sitting in silence for a time, Hrant smiled as he looked at all the homes and other buildings with lots of torches and lanterns flickering throughout the city. He could see the tree-lined main streets and even their own house.

Then Garabed began to speak. "How very peaceful it all appears. Don't you agree, Hrant?" The boy nodded enthusiastically. These had been his thoughts exactly.

"Appearances can be very superficial. We hope for peace. We work hard for peace. We strive daily for peace. We do this with all our neighbors, be they fellow Armenians, Greeks, Jews, Kurds, or Turks. However, peace has been very elusive."

Garabed continued. "Though our ancestors lived here for thousands of years, long before Jesus, the Christ child, was born, we have endured much turmoil and many conquerors. Besides Armenian, our earthly kings have been many... Urartian, Babylonian, Persian,

Roman, Byzantine, and, since the 15th Century, Ottoman.

"Willingly or unwillingly, our bloodlines have mixed for millenniums. But we have remained. We have remained here by Mount Ararat.

"Where we now sit, high on this hill is in part of the Van Fortress, built while Armenians lived under the rule of the Urartu, just a few hundred years before Jesus lived. Fortresses are necessary. They help us prepare to withstand attacks from our enemies. Sadly, we Armenians tend to work so hard we have often failed to foresee evil plans being made by those who would do us harm. Just when we thought we might live peacefully in our Armenian homeland under the Ottoman Empire, a great many of us, many thousands, in fact, were massacred.

"This was shortly before you were born. It happened when your eldest brother, Ohanes, was very close to your age now. However, it is our way... it is our Armenian way... to rise after heartache and injustice to persist, to rebuild, and hold our heads high."

"For thousands of years, we Armenians have lived here at the crossroads of three continents – Africa, Europe, and Asia. While many have ruled us, only the Ottoman Empire seems determined to crush us, rather than let us be. Perhaps it is because we were the first nation to make Christianity our official religion. Perhaps because we honor family, our women, education, and culture.

"Their once powerful Ottoman Empire is now declining. Perhaps they fault us, for they must blame someone other than themselves."

Garabed grew silent. Hrant studied his father's handsome face, flickering with light from the lantern.

He saw great concern there, but also great patience and wisdom.

Hrant truly cherished time alone with his Papa. He could listen to his father talk for hours. This time was different. There was no sparkle in Papa's eye, no hint of a smile at the corner of his lips.

His father resumed speaking. "Our peace is being shattered once again. Though we helped them gain power, the Young Turks gave us false hope and promises. Honest men *keep* their promises. The Young Turks *lied.*

"They are Islamic and do not believe in Jesus Christ. They do not want us to believe in Christ either. Thus, they do not want us to be alive because we are Christian. This intolerance of people who believe differently is challenging to say the least.

"To make matters worse, they are now using the Turkish military and various Muslim tribesmen to drive us from our homes. As you have seen, a great many people have already taken refuge within the walls of Van. Our neighborhoods are swelling rapidly with these people who have lost their homes and their towns. Most of them have lost family members. Many have lost almost everyone they loved."

Hrant looked up at his father. "Will they be safe here, Papa? Will... Will *we* be safe?"

"Ah... with the help of God, yes," the elder Gulumian replied. "Though we want peace, we do not really expect the Ottomans to respect nor spare our precious city. We are in the center of the most fertile soil. These are holy grounds. The Turks have made it rather clear that they do not like the fact that the majority of people in the Van province are Armenians. We have good businesses, architecture, education.

"Since the beginning of man, our lands have been coveted by those seeking power. Our culture, skills, and successes have stirred great envy. For many generations, these attackers have even taken our women to strengthen their own bloodlines, forcing our women to mother the attackers' children. Now the Ottoman Empire is taking from us again. They have attacked so many villages already, and our dear city of Van is a highly prized target. It is just a matter of time.

"Please also remember, Hrant. While the Ottomans commit atrocities against us, we must keep in mind that doing evil things does not require them to be evil people. They are misguided, most assuredly. Leaders tell terrible lies to their Turkish citizens. They repeat horrible misstatements about us as if accepted truths. That is simply how weak and ill-intended political authorities control their people. They employ frequent, if not constant repetition of their desired perception until a great many citizens readily accept it as true, even when it is utterly false.

"No intelligent, rational, or faith-filled people would knowingly or deliberately behave as so many of them are behaving. They have been led astray, lied to about Christians, and pressured by all the powers that be to act out against us. We must not believe that they have evil souls and no love in their hearts. Rather, we need to remember that these Muslims are constantly being taught by their leaders to hate us. We must pray that better judgment will prevail and that they can and will learn to let all people live in peace.

"But son, while we want peace, we are prepared to fight to protect our homes and businesses, to protect the honor of our women, and to preserve a future for Armenia. We have no military. We are small in comparison to the enormous might of the Ottomans. And it has long been considered good advice for a cat to not try to strangle a lion.

"We need help. Our Armenian leaders have been imploring the Europeans and Russians to help us defend ourselves. Regardless, son, with or without outside help, I want you to know that we *will* defend ourselves. Your grandfather and I will fight shoulder to shoulder beside our neighbors. If the Turkish military forces attack, we will be ready.

"While we strive for peace every day, inside every man's heart is a lion that sleeps. They have awakened the lion in all of us. Still, and I repeat myself to make a point you must remember... the Turkish army is much larger and stronger than we are. If they overcome us and breach the wall, your mother will take you and your siblings into the tunnel."

Hrant thought for a moment. "Would the bad men be able to find us in the tunnel, Papa?" Hrant queried softly.

Garabed looked at his young son. The boy's long, wavy, dark locks fluttered about his face in the evening breeze. How deeply Garabed wished he could spare his youngest son from all the hatred and evil in the world. It was not to be.

The elder Gulumian stood up. Hrant followed suit. Garabed's explanation continued as they ever so slowly retraced their steps back into the depths below the Fortress.

"It is true that the bad men could find the tunnel, just as you did, my son. The tunnel is to only be used by you for an emergency escape. You would not come up these steps in the Fortress as we just did. You would follow the other tunnel in that stone room. It connects to the ancient irrigation tunnels and a cave system. Then it comes up outside the walls of Van and away from the fighting. You would then travel north over Mount Ararat toward Yerevan or veer further north to Russia. We will soon decide the best course of action. Then, when the city is secure and life is safe here again, your grandfather and I will come and bring you home."

Now they stood back in the stone room where the tunnel had first brought them. Garabed pointed to the other tunnel opening Hrant had spied earlier.

"That is the way you would go. Your mother knows the way."

Hrant quietly asked, "Papa, how far do these tunnels go?" He watched the flickering lantern light reflected in his father's soft, gray eyes.

Garabed studied his young son's face before answering. "Son, if we are fortunate, you will never have to find out. If we are not fortunate, God will guide you through the tunnels as far as you need to go. Remember, we are Armenians. We are family. We persist. We persevere."

The Coming Storm
15

OVER THE NEXT few weeks there seemed to be a great many evenings when Garabed hosted several of their Armenian friends and neighbors. Interestingly, only one or two men ever came to their door. Many arrived through the stable. Hrant now realized that these were clandestine meetings because most of the men had come to their home through the forbidden, secret tunnel. These evenings were not the festive, music-filled events that Hrant so loved.

Usually, the men huddled around just one or two small torches in the courtyard. They spoke in hushed voices most of the time. Hrant and his siblings were not permitted to join them.

Always seeking to know how things worked, young Hrant quietly sought various places he might secret himself, so he could hear but not get caught. He listened as they whispered about a great war, and about the Ottomans choosing a dangerous partner in a country called Germany. He learned that the unjust poll tax on Armenians had been increased.

By now, all Christian men under age 40, across all Ottoman Empire provinces, had been forced into the Turkish military, though they had been previously forbidden to serve. And Armenians were being required to bring their own weapons, which the men had learned were then being routinely confiscated.

Young Hrant struggled to comprehend this information. The topics discussed by the men came complete with several scenarios that backed up the discomforting news. Evidence of great treachery and evil was mounting. Kurdish criminals were being released from Turkish prisons on the condition that they promised to wreak havoc on the Armenians. This sounded very dangerous and caused Hrant great concern since his father and grandfather were often on the road for several days at a time.

Outside the walls of Van were many Kurdish groups of bandits and landowner warlords. Worse yet was the fact that Papa and Grampa were no longer permitted to travel with weapons to defend themselves.

This was not good news. They were still allowed to travel and do their humanitarian work, but they would no longer have their guns at the ready should they encounter trouble along the roads.

One night, Hrant listened while Papa read the letter that had arrived that week from Hrant's brother, Ohanes, living in Boston in the United States of America. The men gathered by the mulberry tree in their walled courtyard listened intently, as Garabed gently read it aloud by the soft torchlight.

> *"Dearest Family,*
>
> *I know that too many days pass between my writing and you receiving my letters. Urgent news and information are, by now, history.*
>
> *Please know and believe that leaders throughout the civilized world recognize that the Turks are systematically trying to wipe out Armenians. This is not just*

a time of trouble. Tens of thousands have been murdered in villages throughout Armenia. Many unprotected cities have been attacked.

These are no longer isolated incidents. Sadly, you must know that any horror stories you may hear should be multiplied many times. There is no mercy in the Young Turks' hearts. Any effort to protest or beg for time or calmness is considered insurrection.

Anyone who once believed the Young Turks would bring the tolerance they openly advocated must now understand and accept that they lied to us. Repeatedly. There are no other words. They never had any intention to live peacefully with us. They seek nothing less than obliteration. This has been confirmed by high-ranking eyewitnesses. The decision to make Turkey only for Turks is now being enforced. Even the United States Ambassador to the Ottoman Empire, Henry Morgenthau is being quoted regularly in the press here. His accounts and others in the New York Times are nothing less than appalling.

The Russian army is coming to help you. We simply cannot be sure they will get there in time. Without them, you are no match for the size and firepower of the Ottoman army.

Time is not just dear, as Papa is so fond of saying. The time is now. I have said it before, and I say it again. Do not delay. Alert every neighbor and friend.

With all the love in my heart, I beg of you, to please follow the plan. You are my family. You have my heart and my prayers.

With deepest love and respect,
until we meet again,
Ohanes

The men gathered with Garabed and his father in the courtyard nodded in understanding. They already knew all too well of what Ohanes wrote. Small villages and large towns were now being systematically attacked by Ottoman military forces. Five of the six predominantly Armenian provinces had been brutally sacked. Citizens were being murdered or forced from their homes, and their possessions were stolen. Now the massacres had swept far to the east. Van was seriously threatened.

Hrant did not understand how these things could be happening. He listened particularly closely when his father or grandfather spoke, as he knew that they had been out in these villages and had been working hard to help the many refugees.

As usual, several powerful Armenian friends were also there. They, too, had strong political connections and opinions. As discussions grew heated, tempers swirled into the cigarette smoke billowing above them.

"We must take action now," said Aram Manukian. "It is the only way to resist impending massacre." Hrant knew the noted leader was the most respected in Van. The good revolutionary statesman continued.

"The time for more talking and hand-wringing has passed. The Turkish leaders are moving Muslims into Armenian cities further to the east. They are tired of being outnumbered by us in all the Armenian provinces. Now, they are clearing the way to make the Ottoman Empire fully Turkish by annihilating Armenians... our kin!

"Though we, as Armenians, have been divided by our own differing political philosophies, we are now united in our need to survive the Young Turks' terrors. Of course, they are doing their evil under the guise of 'relocating' us, as if we were some poor and needy, minority population in our towns and cities."

"That pretense is merely the beginning," added Dajad Terlemezian. "Repeatedly, we get reports of the men in these towns being murdered almost immediately. Of course, this is to prevent any sort of resistance. To add insult to injury, the Turks are then slaughtering all the young boys. Naturally, they do not want them to grow up and seek revenge for these vicious crimes being perpetrated against Armenians."

Then Hrant heard the men talk about weapons that they had been hiding within the mountain and in the tunnels near the underground water. Oh, dear. Perhaps their tunnel connected to one of these.

And he heard as they continued, these new weapons had been coming from the Russians in hopeful preparation to help them stand up to the Ottoman Empire. The men expressed great gratitude, for these weapons were desperately needed to help replace the many Armenian guns and rifles that had been taken away by the Ottoman authorities.

In fact, in 1908, both Aram Manukian and Dajad Terlemezian had been imprisoned after a traitor revealed the whereabouts of a great many weapons they were hiding from the Turks. Thankfully, they were soon released, as they had helped the Young Turks win their bloodless coups over the Sultan. Still a mere teenager, Dajad became a national hero when he assassinated that traitor.

"Well, the fact that they are now training Armenians and stockpiling weapons again might truly help us," Hrant pondered to himself. All that he had previously heard was the adults bemoaning the fact that all Armenian weapons had been confiscated by the Turks. He had no idea how they were supposed to defend themselves without any weapons. All their talk about standing up to their oppressors and defending their homes had felt rather lacking in substance or means.

Now, he saw a glimmer of hope. New weapons seemed to be at the ready. Perhaps these weapons were already hiding in the tunnels where he had walked with his father. Or maybe they were in some of those side tunnels he observed deep underneath the old fortress. All Hrant could do was imagine.

What he knew was that all this talk and confusion was too much for him to handle in one night. And these meetings were happening nearly every night when his father was home. There was so much information. So much sadness. Great concern. Even fear.

With each conversation, the emotional intensity increased. Hrant's anxiety and confusion grew. Why would their Turkish friends ever hurt them? He could not believe it. He did not *want* to believe it. And yet, an ominous clock seemed to be loudly ticking.

Countdown

16

OTTOMAN MILITARY FORCES gathered outside the walled city of Van. As the days passed, their numbers grew. They lined up many cannons, facing the walls. Plus, they had managed to haul some heavy artillery to the edges of the ancient castle high above the city, providing the perfect strategic advantage. Numerous military sentries stood day and night around every entry gate. They regularly gathered close to streets into Aikesdan, known as the Vineyards, and the largest of the Armenian quarters in Van.

To this point, the army had been allowing certain Armenian tradesmen, refugees, and those with special approval to assist in the refugee assistance efforts to come and go without interference.

There were, of course, thorough searches of all carried packs and loaded wagons to be sure that goods such as food and clothing were not disguising any weapons or other smuggled goods. The Ottoman soldiers were also on the lookout for a great number of Armenian men who were considered threats, as they were deemed leaders who would stir up rebellion.

The military permitted several dozen families to depart from the walled city of Van. Unfortunately, it turned out, with great frequency, these travelers were attacked on the road within mere hours of passing through the gates.

Heavily armed groups of bandits often ended up disappointed to learn that most of these families had already been "relieved" of their valuables by military personnel just outside the walls of the city. The Turks serving with the military forces missed no opportunity to line their own pockets by stealing from the departing citizens.

Armenian refugees from dozens of burned-out villages huddled inside the walls. The Vanetz, the Armenian citizens from Van, brought them food and supplies. Refugees sheltered within homes of friends and families.

Those living in the gardens near the lake's edge had already taken refuge within the walls or had scattered into the mountains or had been slaughtered. Many who lived within the walled city had also opted to pack up their families and take to the roads, despite the heavy risks.

Some such endeavors may have been successful. Positive word rarely came back to friends and family remaining in Van, so it was unknown.

Unfortunately, on a great many occasions, negative, heart-breaking reports came back. Far too often, only the families' desecrated bodies had been found. The stories repeated negative details. Stripped at the side of the road. Murdered. All possessions stolen. Everyone just shook their heads in sorrow.

Many Muslims living in Van also opted to flee, rather than be caught in the inevitable firefight that loomed on the near horizon. They had no argument with their Christian neighbors. Many were good friends. They also relied on the Armenians for goods, services, and the entire marketplace.

But fear spread that the Armenian defenders might mistake them for aggressors. They could also be endangered by their attacking fellow Turkish countrymen. Worse yet, if they did not join the military's effort in removing the Armenians, the forces had orders to evacuate them too, as Armenian sympathizers.

And yet, through it all, Armenians and Turks carried on each day. They worked and tended to their families. They persevered despite the looming threats.

Finally, good news arrived for many of the Armenians' Turkish friends wishing to evacuate. Many ships could now transport them across the great Lake Van if they so desired.

Thankfully, the ships were owned and operated by Armenians, who would give the friendly Turks safe passage. This had not been a worthy possibility prior to this point, as the authorities had been limiting civilian passage in lieu of transporting their military forces.

The shipyards had now decreed that they would no longer carry Turkish military personnel because the government was not willing nor able to pay for these services. The shipyards reported that they would be forced to close completely.

Troops were already in their mandated locations. The government decided that they no longer needed services on Lake Van, at least for the time being, so they agreed.

Thus, with soldiers not on-site to observe civilian Turkish departures across the lake, the friendly Turkish citizens would not be persecuted for consorting with the Armenian infidels. Times were particularly challenging for Muslims known to keep Christian friends. That alone could bring a death sentence to their doors, too.

The Armenians could help save dozens if not hundreds of Turkish families. But what was to happen to the tens of thousands of Armenians still within the walls of Van? Their fate was about to be determined.

No doubt remained. The siege of Van could begin at any moment.

Urgent Preparations
17

HOW ON EARTH could Hrant's family possibly get ready for this great unknown that loomed just around the corner? They did the best they could. Decades later, Cassie wrote in her addendum to her Grandmother Gulumian's memoir about what she had learned regarding this time from her grandfather, Marjorie's husband, Hrant.

"Before leaving with the children for the long trek over Mount Ararat to try to get to safety, my grandfather told me that his mother did one other thing. In hopes of one day returning home, he watched his mother dig big holes in the backyard and bury everything of value that they would not be able to carry with them.

"This even included bolts of fabric and all the sewing notions. Many books were wrapped in canvas before being placed in the earth. Large items, from rugs to musical instruments were given to trusted Turkish friends for safekeeping until they could return following the troubles. They truly thought they'd be able to come home again someday. But the Ottoman insanity was getting worse. The Armenians would never be able to return to their homes in Van."

In truth, Hrant remembered the preparations well. Any remaining letters from Ohanes in the United States were burned. Smaller items were wrapped and buried.

These also included some precious family photographs in their expensively ornate frames. Large items, including the pump organ, a mandolin, other musical instruments, and some large household goods were entrusted to Turkish friends who were well enough connected to the proper government channels that they would not need to flee. Vahram chose to hang onto his violin, as Anush did with her clarinet.

Then their mother involved the four children. She handed a large square of heavy fabric to each child. Aghavni's instructions were clear.

She began, "Pack a pair of extra shoes and outer clothing to walk over the sacred mountain in the snow. We will avoid the deepest snows and the highest peaks, but we will all need to be prepared for pockets of snow and bitter nights, even though it is Spring. Beyond that, choose the three most important personal possessions that you want to have with you."

The children looked at each other quizzically. Could she be serious?

Their mother continued. "Whatever you pack, you must carry. I will also slip a small parcel of bread, cheese, fried meat, dried fruits, and nuts into each parcel, along with a skin of freshwater. This is just in case we get separated. I do not anticipate this, but we must be ready. I will have a large pack of our food supplies and more water."

The boys looked at each other. They both had favorite books, plus their school textbooks for their studies. Could they pack them? It seemed unlikely. What about musical instruments? Various handmade treasures and whittled toys?

Hrant's mind raced. He knew he wanted to keep the special piece of art from his brother, Aram. Oh, and his dear collection of postage stamps. The Ottoman Empire had been one of the first nations in the world to start using adhesive postage stamps back on January 1, 1863. Hrant did not own any stamps that dated back quite that far, but he had a wonderful book in which he had carefully arranged a very wide, time-spanning array, representing several nations, too.

The girls had so many questions. Should they bring their current stitching projects? Or would all the daily work tasks simply cease? Young Anush quickly wondered what would happen to their favorite Van cat, the sleek white beauty with one amber eye and one vivid blue one. She adored the feline she had named Astine, meaning Beauty.

All that the elder sister, Nazeli, could think of was her sweet Toros. What would happen when her fiancé returned and found her gone? Her entire family... gone? She had worked so hard on her dowry items, from a special bed covering and a tablecloth to a lovely baby blanket. Obviously, she needed to pack her wedding dress in her bundle. Nothing beyond that seemed to matter much to her.

Though their minds raced, the four children, Nazeli, Anush, Vahram, and Hrant, all sat quietly as their mother explained another piece of the preparation puzzle. This one drew their complete focus. The possibility had not even crossed their minds.

However, through their close Turkish political connections, Aghavni and Garabed had received a special warning. Armenian boys were not being permitted to live. Babies, sometimes, but not boys. It was paramount that they travel with what would appear to only be girls.

Thus, the two boys would be dressed as girls, complete with shawls to cover their heads. They must also be prepared to *behave* like girls. Too many reports had arrived detailing the murder of young boys to prevent any from growing up and seeking reprisal against the Ottoman Empire.

Nazeli and Anush were loving and dutiful sisters. They immediately began working with their young brothers to help them learn basic skills that had previously seemed automatic to them. The boys would not understand such nuances as casting their eyes downward, or clutching their shawls close to their bodies, or tilting their heads a bit in constant deference.

They never once even thought of giggling or making light of the situation, as they helped their mother slip the female garments over the wide-eyed boys for the first of several rehearsals. Mama had made the dresses in secret, without the girls even knowing. Aghavni had been preparing for some time.

There were also a couple of guns, along with ammunition. Papa would keep one. He had trained Aghavni to readily handle the other. These items, along with their ammunition, had been hidden in the vegetable cellar.

After the government demanded all weapons be turned in to local authorities, the family had secreted these two guns away. They knew they needed them for both safety and emergency use. Regardless, guns were now considered to be illegal weapons. The Gulumians did not care.

Garabed knew that no good could come of a government disarming its citizens. They would be left at the whim of merciless rulers... officials who claimed to respect the Armenians but then issued orders that directly disavowed their many, hollow promises. This situation boded badly for these peace-loving people.

The Gulumians, just as the other Armenian families, knew that giving up all their weapons would be akin to giving up all hope of freedom. At the very least, they would need weapons just to stay alive as they tried to escape to safety in Russia.

Escaping the city without getting caught was just the first step. The family also needed to be prepared to deal with bandits, both along the roads and off the roads. Plus, there were numerous natural perils in the mountains. Avoiding Turkish military personnel was, perhaps, the easy part.

Hrant remembered being most impressed with how organized and calmly matter of fact their mother was about it all. She was fully organized. She was prepared. Strong. Serene.

She then revealed some petticoats she had fashioned for herself and their daughters. Oh, yes. Even the two newest "daughters" would each have a customized petticoat. She had sewn a variety of pockets into each one. Coins and jewelry items had been placed in the pockets. Then intricate stitches or ties allowed each pouch to be securely closed.

Additional groups of coins were individually stitched into the hems of each petticoat. The children marveled at how hard their mother had been working and completely in secret.

No matter what happened, each would have money and items of value that could be sold to help them survive. One pocket for each of them contained a sort of map. In truth, it just featured a few names. One list had names of landmarks, rivers, towns, villages, monasteries, and cities. Passing by or through each one would help them all end up at the same destination in Russia.

There were also the names of a couple of people to seek out once in Russia. These were people who could help contact Ohanes and Aram in the United States. These contacts could even get them to a ship to America, if necessary, where they would find their elder brothers.

This, of course, was only a worst-case scenario preparation. The goal was to stay in Russia until the troubles settled down. Then Garabed would help the family return home to Van and peacefully resume their lives once again.

Woah. These were a lot of impossibilities lumped into one evening, right? Wrong. This was about their survival. They were fortunate. They *had* possibilities. Some people had nowhere to go nor any planned safe landing place.

Nothing would be easy, but they could do this. They *had* to do this. Whatever "this" turned out to be.

They were ready, right? They were prepared to travel as a family and fight their way to safe harbors, wherever that might take them. Papa's final plan focused on trekking further north and west of Yerevan to cross the Russian border. He feared that if Van fell, the Turks might simply continue their eastward trek. Yerevan could be next.

Other family members had settled on the Mediterranean coast, but that area had fallen early to the evil Ottoman treachery. So, the actual planned escape route would take the Gulumian family north over the sacred mountain of Ararat to reach Kars in Russia. Garabed and his father specifically selected Kars because of its demographics. Armenians constituted nearly fifty percent of the population, followed by Russians and Greeks.

Plans were ready. Now they merely awaited the signal to proceed. Garabed led them as a family. He would know exactly what to do and when to do it. Aghavni and the children were as poised and as prepared as possible. In truth, who on earth could have been prepared for what was about to happen?

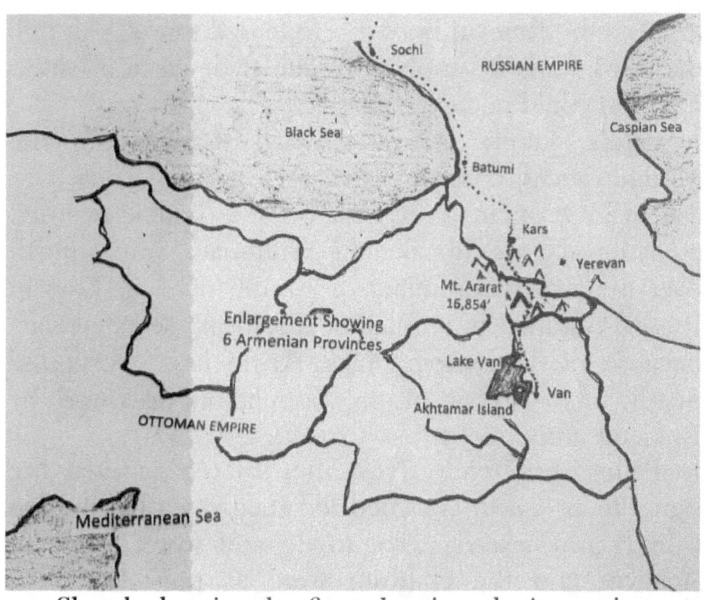

Sketch showing the 6 predominantly Armenian provinces, Lake Van, and Mount Ararat, near what was then the Russian border

Normalcy
18

ANOTHER NIGHT WITH her husband away from home. Aghavni knew their work was vital, but oh! How deeply she hoped these stress-filled times would end soon.

As she thought about her beloved Garabed, Aghavni slipped her wedding ring off her finger. He taught her well that it would serve no good purpose to wear anything that the Ottomans might see and want to steal. She had sewn a special pocket for it, so it could travel close to her heart. Before she hid it there, she took a moment to enjoy its delicate beauty one last time.

So many years ago, Garabed had chosen for her a wedding ring that was a trio of pure gold bands. The center one featured two golden hearts, symbolizing their enjoined hearts. Topping each of the two outside rings was a gold hand, representing their actual hands.

When the three bands folded together, the two hands clasped together perfectly, directly over the hearts. This possession was easily her most dearly treasured. She fondly recalled his sweet words when Garabed presented it to her at their wedding.

"My bride," he began. "If you are willing to take my hand and walk with me through life, I promise you that I will always be true. As our hands join now, our hearts will also join in love." Garabed had been so right.

She stitched the secret little pocket in her blouse securely closed. Aghavni also made a quiet vow that she would always wear the ring near her heart. Sadly, it seemed unsafe to wear it on her finger any longer during these times of deep trouble. Aghavni sighed.

She had just now finished the last of the night's sewing work. The men from Garabed's shop would come in the morning and pick up the completed items to take to the shop. They would arrive early, just after the sun rose, as usual.

Aghavni was grateful that their employees were also friends. Whenever Garabed needed to travel, these men immediately picked up the slack.

Normally, Garabed and her father-in-law, the elder Ohanes, transported all items, bringing new work home to the ladies at the end of each day. While away, their friends brought work for the ladies each morning and picked up the completed work to take to the shop. Under their Turkish rulers, women were not permitted to even walk through the streets unescorted. Everyone was grateful the other tailors were willing to help with the risky exchanges.

So, Aghavni prepared, just as she did every evening. She bundled together her work and the pieces her daughters had brought down to her just a few minutes earlier.

She pictured her golden wedding ring with the two hands clasped at the center. Garabed always reminded her when he departed on these trips that she only needed her ring to remember that no matter where he might be, he was always with her. He always would be holding her hand, even if time and distance meant he could only hold her hand in his heart.

Garabed had it made especially for her. This ring beautifully symbolized his love. It became the physical embodiment of their shared love and their family. Aghavni knew that if she could save but one possession, there was no question. Her wedding ring must always be with her.

Now she could hear the girls playing their musical instruments. They all loved music. How sad Aghavni felt that they would be leaving most of the instruments behind with Turkish friends for safekeeping.

The boys now chimed in with the girls. Vahram played his oud and Hrant sang his little heart out, whenever he set his flute aside, that is.

She then started hearing Hrant's voice lilting out into the street. Aghavni knew he had stepped out onto the front balcony, as he so loved to do. His sweet, clear tones softly flowed into the night. Neighbors had often commented about how much they loved hearing his singing, reverberating down the nearby streets. Now she thought about how their friends would miss his singing.

She admitted to herself that she would miss these moments when Hrant would simply step outside and start to sing. He needed no audience. It was as if he simply raised his voice and sang to God.

It became hard to imagine silence at all in this formerly busy little neighborhood. Little did she know that the silence was doomed to be deafening, as it echoed the local hushing of a generation.

Aghavni could not worry about that. In her own family, she frequently worried about Vahram. He was a good lad, but he was far smaller than he should be at his age. Doctors had believed earlier that he would overcome the challenges they diagnosed shortly after his birth. His mind was sharp, but his body remained frail.

Vahram had grown quite skillful at baking bread in their large courtyard oven. This could be a useful trade for him. However, Aghavni knew that standing for long hours on his feet was never good for the boy.

On the other hand, both daughters inspired confidence. They easily breezed through their home studies for schooling. They had become proficient in several languages, including Turkish and French. They had even learned a little English and had written a couple of letters to their brother Ohanes in English to prove it.

As females, they knew not to let outsiders become aware that they both spoke and understood Turkish, Kurdish, or any other foreign language. That would indicate higher education and get the family in great trouble.

Regardless, even without attending additional school classes in person, they were just as fluent as their brothers. They knew more languages, as only the girls had also started to learn English.

Further, the girls had not shirked their home skills in the process. Aghavni knew they would both be wonderful wives, homemakers, and mothers one day.

On this evening, Aghavni simply closed her eyes and listened. Her children made her smile.

Now and then they stopped making music. Then the air filled with chatter and laughter, until once again they started playing and singing.

Ah, yes. She felt mightily blessed. Aghavni said a quiet prayer of thanks for her loving husband, beautiful family, and more than comfortable home.

As with all Armenian families, they had faced many hardships, but they shared great love and happiness, too. No one could ever take these memories away. Even though she knew that now they would have to travel away for a time, Aghavni recognized that would only be until the current swell of Turkish troubles settled down.

This was their home. Family had lived here for many generations. They would hold their heads high with the knowledge that God would bring them home again.

Little did she know that this night would be the last one for gathering sweet memories for a very long time. Opposing memories brewed nearby.

Photo courtesy of J. Plenio

Worst Nightmares

19

THE URGENT KNOCKING on the door awakened the entire household. In truth, Aghavni had long been up and about. She had heeded the late-night courier's message.

"Aghavni, my dove, time is dear. Time is near." That was all her husband's note needed to say. She hurriedly made the final preparations.

The family knew by this message that they had just a few short hours left. They were quickly packed, dressed, and ready to depart as soon as Garabed and his father returned.

Her husband had frequently and lovingly referred to Aghavni as "my dove," which she knew was the meaning of her name. She also knew that if he ever wrote it in a message, it meant she must prepare the family to "fly" away immediately. "Time is near" also meant he was close.

She had awakened the children, and they all were ready. They awaited Papa's arrival in the main room.

Meanwhile, the children had grown weary and dozed off where they sat, though the sun had risen a couple of hours earlier, and the tailors had already picked up the completed sewing.

Now, the children all woke up instantly. Aghavni had rushed to the door and flung it open.

Rubbing the sleep from his eyes, Hrant could hear a man talking with his mother at a frantic pace. He recognized the voice, but he could not immediately identify it. Then her agonized scream cut through the silence of the previously calm morning.

As all four children rushed toward their mother, they saw Garin Atamian helping her back into the room. He was a long-time family friend and among the merchants that had been traveling with their father and grandfather.

Everyone sat in stunned silence as he explained the ambush details and reiterated his deep sorrow at the murders of their loved ones. News of such loss could never be delivered easily. But these were dear friends. They were like family to him. Tears flowed down everyone's cheeks.

Garabed and Ohanes had been so close to getting home to their family. Now, instead of standing shoulder to shoulder to resist their oppressors and trying to help loved ones evacuate, they were gone.

The family now saw even greater danger looming large. Having heard Aghavni's scream, several neighbors quickly gathered at the door. They offered heartfelt condolences before rushing back to their homes to also ready their families. They may hide. They might run. They could prepare to fight.

For the Gulumians, there would be no time for mourning. A surrealistic trance billowed and enveloped them all.

Garin Atamian then hurried off to share the tragic news with the other victims' families. The wolf had indeed arrived at their door.

No one knew exactly what to expect. However, this turn of events had not entered their minds.

Aghavni quietly closed the front door and turned to her four children. She squared her shoulders and lifted her chin, feigning the most courage she could muster. Inside, she felt this could not be real. There must be some wretched mistake. On the outside, she exuded pure survival mode.

"It's just us now. Our hearts are broken, but we must not let our spirits break, too. Papa had warned us about the organized evacuations. At whatever risk and whatever cost, we must not leave our city in one of those. However, we must leave... now... without delay."

Aghavni quietly continued, reminding herself as much as the children. "Armenians are born survivors. We have been subjected to atrocities, murder, foreign domination, hardships, and natural disasters. But we persevere. We survive. We rebuild."

The next urgent pounding at the door hardly surprised the family. So many friends and neighbors had been stopping by to share their grief over the ambush and the pending attack they all now knew could not be held back any longer.

Aghavni glanced at her wide-eyed brood. Heading to the door she calmly said, "Gather your things now, my dears. We depart through the stable when these friends leave. We will come back home when the trouble ends."

The brothers and sisters immediately scrambled to follow her instructions. They moved to make a quick final check in their rooms, partially to see if they mistakenly left some treasure behind, and partially to take one final look at their personal spaces and belongings before departing.

Back in the main room, Mother opened the door. What greeted her broadened her eyes and stopped her heart for an instant.

A group of uniformed soldiers clustered at the door. Now they attempted to enter. She stood firmly, blocking their way. The burly one at the front started barking insults and loud commands. Aghavni resolutely stated they had no right to enter her home.

He screeched at her, "YOU have no rights at **all**!" The leader then drew his pistol and fired a warning shot into the air. He pushed brusquely past her into the center of the room. The other soldiers followed him. The raging insults continued.

They swiftly moved from room to room, pulling the children into the main room. They barked orders to gather all valuables immediately in preparation for relocation to "safer" areas.

Mother tried to explain that they had no valuables. All the soldiers needed to do was look around them. It seemed true, at least for outward appearances. Rugs no longer lay on the floors, tapestries and other works of art no longer adorned the walls, and not as much as a candlestick sat on the sparse remaining furniture.

In preparation, Aghavni had previously stored all rugs, some furniture, and other larger items of value with those Turkish friends who were well connected and would not need to evacuate if fighting broke out. She had also buried many of their possessions and tailoring supplies in the backyard. Naturally, they planned to return to their home when this trouble subsided.

Aghavni knew they would continue their successful tailoring business. That is the Armenian way. Survive. Rebuild. Persevere.

But the men shoved her and the two youngest "girls" into a corner, pointing guns and swords at them. Their various travel packs had been dropped to the floor in the hectic skirmish.

Mother held the two young boys close to her, pushing them behind her. Dressed in girls' clothing and headscarves, they appeared too young to rape. Thus, they were spared. However, had the soldiers known they were actually boys, they most likely would have been slaughtered on the spot.

Based on the accusations being hurled, Aghavni quickly figured the situation out. These men must have been among the troops who had ambushed her husband and father-in-law just a few short hours earlier. They had come to punish Garabed's family and make of them a harsh example for other Armenians. She very much wanted to leap on them and scratch their eyes out. But, no. Survive!

As soon as the ruckus had started, she had noticed young Anush slip out the back door into the courtyard. She would be hiding near her favorite urn and tree, no doubt. Good. Let her avoid these fiends.

Delicate Nazeli stood frozen in the center of the room. Her state of shock snapped when one of the soldiers threw her over his shoulder and headed into the courtyard.

Aghavni was now screaming at the soldiers and clawing to get past them to her daughter. One soldier hit her hard with a backhand that dropped her to the floor like a rag doll.

She slowly regained her wits and balance. She arose. Aghavni sternly ordered her young boys to stay perfectly still and utterly quiet.

Then she harshly whispered, "No matter what happens, you do not move! You do NOT move."

Hearing Nazeli wailing in the courtyard, Aghavni knew she had to get out there. Then came the scream from Anush.

The brutes had both girls and were tearing the clothing from their bodies. The girls were fighting back with all their might, but they were no match for the soldiers pinning them down and attacking them.

As Aghavni tried to push through the door, a soldier threw her to the floor and slammed the butt of his rifle down on her left hand, crushing three fingers.

She continued her verbal railing of the attackers. The soldier's boot grinding into her bleeding hand kept her from her efforts to help stop the assault on her daughters.

She called out to them. "Survive this! Just survive these beasts."

By the time the second and third savages were raping Nazeli, the teenager had grown silent. Tears flowed down her face, but she had given up the fight.

Not Anush. The spirited younger daughter continued to defiantly twist and turn, shriek and scream... that is, until the single gunshot rang out, forever silencing her.

Aghavni wailed the agonizing cry only a mother could understand. But, on the ground beside her slain sister, Nazeli merely whimpered in shock, pain, and horror.

The moments continued passing in grotesque slow motion. The final soldier abusing Nazeli stood up. He scratched his head. He wiped a splatter of Anush's blood from his cheek. Then he spit on Nazeli, just before he drew his pistol and shot her.

These soldiers had just brutally raped the two sisters. The fiends had laughed jubilantly as they shot them, declaring them guilty of fighting back and defying their orders. Their **orders!?!**

Hrant's favorite sister had just barely turned 14. Now she and her 17-year-old older sister lay dead on the ground.

The soldiers turned their attention now to Aghavni and the two remaining youngsters. They ordered the remnants of the family to accompany them to the town center. They would be escorted along with some others to safer places.

Hah! *THEY* would escort them. *Safer* places? These same monsters had just vilely assaulted and murdered Nazeli and Anush. How could anyone possibly believe they spoke a sincere word about anything?

Aghavni recalled Garabed's warnings about the horrors of these caravans. They should have simply called them what they were... death marches. The Ottomans let Armenians die on the roads, murdered them outright, invited bandits and villains to attack at will, sold girls into harems, and drove the surviving few into bleak camps in the Syrian desert. Further, the Ottoman Turks had no intention of anyone enduring those camps for long.

Relocation to safer places? Hardly! Their home and city had been perfectly safe until Ottoman soldiers turned into thugs and gave in to their bloodlust!

Aghavni and the boys crumbled in total shock. All three of them were visibly trembling and shaking uncontrollably. They were angry, hurt, and frightened. They were heartbroken beyond definition.

"All right, let's move them along." A familiar voice rang out as Serkan Raffi came through the door. He was a Turkish soldier but also a family friend.

Of course, he hardly seemed to be acting as their friend now. Quite the opposite. Aghavni could hardly believe that he would join this group of soldiers in their heinous plans.

Serkan continued, "We have our orders directly from the ruling triumvirate of the Young Turks. The provincial governors throughout Turkey are following their instructions. You must leave these provinces now. This is for your safety."

The hideous roundups were beginning here in their precious walled city of Van. They would not be spared. Outlying villages had already fallen. With Van, this eastern Armenian province would soon be under an all-out siege.

Aghavni knew they would not have dared breach her door had the Gulumian home been within the area surrounded by the trenches already dug by resistance forces. Sadly, their home had vulnerability as it sat amidst a few other homes just beyond the trenched sections. Trenches were at outer areas, and certainly not in those with the secret tunnels.

Serkan Raffi's tone was commanding, as he thanked the soldiers. He assured the men that he would take over now and bring this family to the square.

Serkan then entered the now bloodied courtyard, the same yard where even he had spent many pleasant nights of music and merriment. The horrific scene he beheld broke his heart.

As soon as the others were outside and out of sight, Serkan dropped his pretense and wrapped his arms around Aghavni with sincere condolences. He begged her to not hate them all for the evil the Ottoman soldiers had perpetrated against her family on this day.

Oh, yes. He revealed his awareness of the ambush and murders of her husband and father-in-law also. Of course, he failed to mention the little detail that he had been a personal eyewitness to that early dawn surprise attack or that he had made no attempt to stop it or even speak up on their behalf.

Raffi then quickly explained that he had been down the street when he had heard the gunshots. He ran their way as quickly as he could. However, now he had no choice but to take them to the square to meet the others, mostly refugees. He also looked her in the eye as he warned Aghavni to NOT step through the West or South gates of Van into the countryside.

"These evacuation marches are very dangerous," he added. "Do whatever you have to do, but you must try to take cover elsewhere. Run. Hide. But, whatever you do, do not return to this house.

"I will visit your clergymen. I will personally see to it that the bodies of your beloved daughters are properly handled from this point forward. I am so, so sincerely sorry that all this unspeakable horror has happened to you, wonderful people. You cannot possibly imagine my remorse. Somehow, I must make this up to you. Somehow. Someday. I promise."

With that, Serkan ushered Aghavni, Vahram, and Hrant out their front door, and closed it behind them. As he walked the stunned trio to the square, he pretended to not even notice that the two boys were completely dressed as girls. He had watched them growing up and knew perfectly well that they were boys.

In his mind, Serkan realized the family must have been preparing to make a run for it. How he wished they had succeeded!

Serkan lowered his head a bit and spoke quietly to Aghavni. "There is much you don't know. Though I am one, I must caution you to trust no Turks at this time.

"Run, do not walk away from this mess. Please. I beg of you. With God's help, this trouble will pass. Your heartbreak is beyond measure on this day. I know not how we can ever make these tragedies up to any of you."

As they entered the square, he raised his voice to full volume. "Fill your wineskins with water. The road ahead is a long one."

With that, Serkan Raffi turned and vanished into the crowd of soldiers. He was gone.

Aghavni, Vahram, and Hrant stood still. A surreal sense of total numbness overtook them, from the sheer horror they had just experienced.

Now or Never
20

AGHAVNI UTTERED MANY silent prayers. She especially prayed for the souls of her husband, her father-in-law, and her two precious daughters. She also made a silent promise. She would do whatever it took to protect her two little boys. As any mother would feel, she made a total commitment to getting them out of this terror alive. Somehow.

The little family was granted no time to grieve. They had just lost Garabed and his father. They had just lost Nazeli and Anush. They had just been forced from their own home.

Survival became the sole focus. Their faces all reflected the same ashen daze of despair.

Still, Aghavni wondered why just a few dozen families had been singled out for this first forced "relocation?" Perhaps it was because their few houses were just outside the trenches dug by the Armenian resistance. Perhaps it was because they were all that remained of families of men the Ottoman soldiers had recently slaughtered. She knew her family had been specifically selected. The others could merely have had their luck run out.

Some were refugees, already displaced here after their villages had been destroyed. She could not help but feel the wretched hopelessness in their faces. They had survived unspeakable horrors in their own towns and villages, only to come here to see matters growing worse.

This would surely be a way of warning other Armenians. They were being made an example of to deliver a crystal-clear message. The soldiers wanted to continue punishment for what they viewed as Armenian revolution efforts.

Resistance and the mere desire for equality or some semblance of autonomy were viewed as insurrection. Reasons mattered little. Reason and logic no longer existed.

Soldiers channeled the small group of Armenian women, children, and elderly into a line. They continued chastising their prisoners for being traitors, berating them for being friendly to England and Russia. Both those nations had sided against Germany, with which the Ottoman Empire had formally aligned itself in the ongoing war.

It was true that Armenians had a positive relationship with England. Britain was home to many respected universities and great art museums. Armenians considered it an honor to send children to study there and be exposed to western culture and art. Of late, England had made it clear that the atrocities being committed against the Armenians by the Ottomans would not be tolerated.

Russia always remained a sore subject for the Ottoman Empire. Both nations had great interest in these lands around the Caucasus Mountains. The Ottomans suspected that after confiscating guns from their Armenian subjects, the Russians had been secreting new weapons to the Armenians to help in resistance efforts in the Van Province.

Yet, the authorities and Turkish soldiers had failed to find these new weapons. The Russian Empire, meanwhile, made it clear that it was not a fan of the growing extermination and deportation endeavors being carried out by the Turks against the Armenians.

So, having nations sympathetic to their plight also made the Armenians true revolutionaries in the eyes of the Ottoman Turkish government. Stirring strong anti-Christian sentiments among civilian populations, made it even easier for the Ottoman soldiers and their mercenaries to carry out their inhumane plans.

As Aghavni pondered their situation, she was suddenly startled. A soldier started yelling behind them. He and several others started pushing and shoving any Armenians that were still sitting to get to their feet. Some officer barked the order for them to get walking and stay in line.

When she looked up to see who had spoken, anger flashed through her eyes. The young officer sat upon her husband's elegant horse. Mitan was impossible to miss. His glossy black coat was not mistakable amidst the golden color of the other fine Armenian horses. But this oaf in uniform was even using Garabed's saddle. She turned away and spat on the ground.

The last three remaining in the Gulumian family in Van began walking in a quiet parade toward certain doom. Soldiers with bayonets fastened at the ends of their rifles now escorted the group of Armenians through the city streets toward the South or Middle Gate.

Dusk had fallen, and shadows loomed larger than life. An eerie mask of quiet enveloped the houses like some foreboding fog. Anyone hiding within nearby walls hardly dared to breathe, fearing getting dragged from their homes and added to the forced deportation march.

They now entered the Turkish quarter, and Aghavni knew she only had a limited number of streets to pass before they would reach the Middle Gate, located on the southern side of the walled city. Remembering Serkan Raffi's warning to not pass through it, nor return to their home, she quickly considered her few options.

Either she must risk it all and run with the boys, or they would have to take their chances with the soldiers and throngs of bandits outside the walls. Even if they could remain relatively safe on this night, being stripped of their clothing and belongings would reveal to the soldiers that Vahram and Hrant were *not* little girls after all. Their disguises would be for naught. They would all surely be slaughtered where they stood.

Mother had quietly alerted her sons that when she squeezed their hands two times quickly in succession that meant they were to run with her immediately. Both had nodded. They trusted her.

Aghavni chose a specific street because she recalled from earlier excursions that it curved after a very short block and then it branched. She thought this might give them a chance to confuse the soldiers long enough to find a hiding place.

Now, with the closest armed guard facing forward, though just mere feet in front of them, she squeezed the boys' hands two times. On her signal, they all swiftly turned to the right and scurried as quickly and quietly as possible into the far alley.

Neither Hrant nor Vahram dared look back. As soon as they darted between the buildings, the trio started to run.

Almost immediately, Hrant heard the yelling of one of the Ottoman guards, but they did not stop. They did not slow down. Despite her freshly wounded left hand, Mother gripped their hands even tighter and ran even faster. Finally, they cleared the outskirt buildings, only to hear gruff Turkish yelling from down yet another street.

They were being ordered to stop, but they did not look back, never mind slow their pace or stop. The angry, yelling voice drew closer. Hrant kept running, as fast as his foolish skirt permitted. At the same time, he knew they would all most assuredly be struck down by the broad Ottoman sword within minutes or even moments.

Vahram struggled to breathe. He could not run any further. His mother scooped the little lad up, wrapped under one of her arms. She did not even break her stride, but she certainly could not keep up this pace while carrying him for much longer. Yes, he was very small for his age, but she already had filled sacks of supplies strapped to her back, plus she now bore his weight and his filled parcel. This was a highly determined mother, who managed to somehow summon seemingly superhuman strength.

As they darted around another corner, Aghavni pulled Hrant and Vahram behind a large pile of bricks. They instinctively ducked down, huddled closely together.

Their mother swept her large, dark shawl up over them all. The construction rubble provided slight cover at best, but they had to stop.

Underneath the shawl, Aghavni held Vahram close to her body, hoping her clothing would muffle his wheezing. The angry Turkish ranting voice drew closer.

They sat perfectly still hoping the encroaching darkness would shield them.

Unfortunately, the little lad moved his foot and struck a stack of bricks. A pail tumbled down, hitting the street with a crash. Vahram squeezed his mother's hand. She held the two boys tight and still. She closed her eyes and awaited their fate.

"Ah-hah!" The soldier bellowed out from mere feet away. They heard his deep, guttural snarl as he approached their hiding spot. "So, I have found you stubborn, Armenian dogs," he sarcastically hissed. "You thought you could hide from me! Hah!"

Just then a Van cat leaped up onto the top of the construction material, with its fluffy white tail waving proudly. The Gulumians had not even seen the cat when they hurriedly hunkered down.

"Meee-owww!" The Van cat cooed enticingly. It tilted its head and looked at the huge soldier inquisitively.

"Awww, kahretsin!!! Dammit," the Turk squawked. "Just a damn cat!"

He turned and headed off in the direction from which he had come. The family could hear him angrily sputtering as he moved into the distance and rounded a far corner.

Aghavni paused a few more seconds, before slowly lifting an edge of her giant shawl. It was quite dark now, but they could see the fluffy white feline that had just saved them. The mystical Van cat, very much like the one in their neighborhood that Anush had nicknamed "Beauty," with its classic one blue and one gold eye, now sat looking down at them, still tilting its head from side to side.

Hrant believed the cat was smiling. It seemed quite pleased with itself for having thwarted the soldier without so much more than a "meow."

Aghavni stooped to pick up their small sacks. The boys stood up beside her and each took his sack. Vahram's breathing was still quite labored. She needed to find him a safe place to lie down.

Could they somehow get into the Van Fortress high above them? Several pathways meandered up the rocks to the castle on top, but they could surely become trapped up there. Ottoman soldiers were already stationed on the huge rock.

Could they possibly make it through one of the other gates unnoticed? Unlikely, but that was the only way she knew to get to the monastery.

Aghavni knew that the tunnels held ample supplies and a sure exit. What she did not know is how they could gain access without going back to their home. Besides, for all they knew, the soldiers may have already found their trap door entrance.

Home. As she stood virtually frozen in one spot, Aghavni thought about her precious daughters lying dead on the ground in their own yard. Could she be sure that Serkan Raffi would properly take care of them? Well, she had to believe that he would, especially if he enlisted help from any of her few remaining neighbors or the priests.

"Pssst!" Startled, Aghavni spun around toward the quiet voice they had just heard. Framed in soft light, she could see the silhouette of a woman peering out from a doorway across the alley. The woman was motioning for them to come to her.

The cat was already leading the way. The trio nervously followed.

A Van cat
Photo courtesy of Nicolas Flor

Hope from Within
21

MANY YEARS LATER, when Hrant's aging wife in America journaled about these difficult experiences, she captured the sense of these horrific times and the confusion they inspired. Among the notes later published with the memoir were these thoughts from Cassie on the cultural clash that nearly wiped out the Armenians.

"I understand what we today call 'spin' has come from the modern Turkish government and their historians. They, naturally, wish to gloss over this barbaric time in their development. There was much chaos with World War I. Armenians were living throughout the Ottoman Empire. The ethnic differences between the Turks and the Armenians were large, especially based on the Armenians' Christian faith in a sea of Muslim sects. The two primary other differences, according to Hrant and what he learned from his family, were the facts that Armenians prided themselves on developing intellectual strengths and believed strongly in education. And, secondly, they did not belittle nor diminish women.

"Even today, I have listened with sadness, whenever I have heard Turks in America downplay the million-and-a-half to two million Armenian deaths at the hands of the Ottomans as just "hype." They have been taught, and it has been repeated for emphasis, that this poor minority ethnic group was merely being relocated for its own protection. Correcting their constantly brainwashed perception does little to even crack the surface of their defensive posture.

"Well, that happened *after* what was left of Hrant's family made its daring escape. Thankfully, the family did not go the way the Turkish government herded the other women, children, and elderly. Along with hundreds of thousands of fellow Armenians, those poor souls were often murdered or left to starve or die of dehydration."

For now, the remaining Gulumian family was trapped in Van. While they dared not trust anyone, especially anyone who was Turkish, at this moment they felt little choice.

As they stepped into the dimly lit little room, the woman shocked them. She spoke in perfect Armenian. "Please do not be afraid. I will not hurt you. I am Armenian by birth. My name is Arexi."

Aghavni heard herself breathe a heavy sigh of relief. They were safe... at least for now.

"Could you perhaps spare a sip of water for my young son here?" Aghavni continued, "He has great difficulty breathing."

"Goodness, yes!" Arexi moved quickly, getting Vahram some water and helping him to sit down. The woman had not hesitated, although Aghavni had just called one of the little girls her son.

Then the two women started talking in earnest. They shared and learned a great deal from each other.

Arexi and her older brother had been living as Turks since their parents had died in the "troubles" years earlier. She was just a toddler then.

A friendly Turkish family had taken them in and changed their names to help disguise their true identities. Arexi was her Armenian name. They had been living on their own now for two years.

Her brother, Tavit, also his Armenian name, made sure she learned the Armenian language and never let her forget who she really was. For quite some time, he had been secretly working with the Armenian resistance.

She expected her brother to be home any time now. Arexi assured Aghavni that he would know what to do to help them escape.

Awaiting his return, Arexi served the little family and tried to make them as comfortable as possible. Aghavni shared with her what had transpired over this horrific day. Well, she shared the story, but she deliberately and respectfully left out the most inhumane details. When she finished, Arexi wrapped her arms around the sad mother. Both women wept openly.

And yet, no. Aghavni could not let herself break down. The shock of the day's events may or may not have been wearing off. She was not sure. She was sure that none of it should have happened. She also knew that Garabed would want her to be strong. She had to be strong for Vahram and Hrant. She had to be strong for the souls of Nazeli and Anush.

Aghavni now stood tall. She straightened up and squared her shoulders. Lifting her chin, she knew the responsibilities of the family fell to her. There was no time to grieve. She needed to be strong for them all.

So much hatred had caused immeasurable pain and grief already. Why couldn't the Ottomans just let the Armenians live in peace? Everything felt far beyond possible comprehension.

Aghavni looked at Arexi with great gratitude. She could not help but marvel at the courage shown by such a young woman. Arexi could not have been much older than her own Nazeli. She recognized the same glow of gentle kindness in Arexi that she had adored in her daughter.

Just then, as promised, Tavit arrived. Arexi introduced her brother to Aghavni and shared the little family's story. His eyes grew dark, and his brow furrowed. Then Tavit turned to Aghavni.

"Aghavni. Oh, Aghavni. I knew Garabed well," he began. "He was a good man and highly respected, as was your father-in-law. He was a calm and strong leader. You have our deepest condolences.

"We, in the resistance, have just finished meeting on this very subject. To find you here now, I count as a blessing. All that has transpired in these past 24 hours initiated our hasty meeting. We were informed of all the evil you and your family endured. Everyone is heartbroken. The men pray for you all. They man the trenches as we speak.

"You also have my word that I will do anything and everything in my power to help you and your children safely escape. I promise you."

Aghavni bowed her head and murmured, "Thank you, Tavit. Thank you, Arexi. You are both a most amazing blessing for us at this time."

"Speaking of time," Tavit interjected. "We must prepare to move quickly and silently. You will have to wear a veil to appear as a Turkish woman, especially in this Turkish quarter.

"The soldiers are looking for one Armenian woman with two children. They will not look twice at a Turkish man with two women and two children.

"Turkish forces are growing ever larger outside the walls, with a great many cannons. My sister and I will not be staying here either, because the dangers are growing too rapidly.

"Our provisions are already stowed underground. But for now, we will all rest. Try to get some sleep because you may not have that opportunity again for many hours. We move at first light."

Photo courtesy of Andrew Neel

On the Move
22

LED BY TAVIT, the little group moved smoothly through the Turkish neighborhood, heading in a northerly direction, back toward Aikesdan, the Armenian quarter. Tavit had smartly packed the Gulumians' little parcels into one bundle, which he carried, so the family would not appear as travelers.

"Baris! Baris!" A husky man across the street called out.

"Oh, no," thought Aghavni. "We have been found out!"

"Günaydin! Good morning, Berk!" Tavit feigned great glee as he called back in Turkish to the large man, who had stopped and appeared to be about to cross the street to join them.

Tavit lowered his voice to a whisper now. "Just keep walking. Do not change pace or look up."

He then waved at Berk. "We will return shortly. I will stop by," he said loudly, in perfect Turkish. He hoped to stop the man from coming closer. His ploy seemed to have worked. The desperate little group scurried on its way.

"Baris is the Turkish name our family's friends gave me when they took Arexi and me in after we lost our parents following the Hamidian massacres. But I just lied to Berk. We will not be returning shortly, and I have no plans to 'stop in' to chat with him ever again."

Well into the Armenian neighborhood now, Tavit suddenly steered the group to the doorway of a home. The door opened quite quickly after he knocked.

"I did not expect so many of you," the elderly woman inside uttered. She stepped aside, clearing the doorway for them to swiftly enter past her.

She then looked outside in the street, subtly turning her head to glance cautiously in both directions. Seeing no people whatsoever in any direction, she then immediately closed the door behind them.

"My most sincere apologies, Mariam," said Tavit. "My sister managed to rescue this family from the soldiers just last night. The rest of their family has been killed by the Turks. Please, this is Aghavni Gulumian, Garabed's wife. We had no way to alert you."

"Aghavni!" Mariam's voice raised considerably. Now she looked directly at Aghavni as she continued.

"I am deeply honored to meet you. I have long admired your work for the Women's Union. You inspired me to get involved in helping make and collect items for refugees also. There is no one I could be more honored to help than you."

"You give me far too much credit," responded Aghavni. "I am just one of many who work to help our people. I deeply thank you for *your* assistance."

"Good ladies," interrupted Tavit. "While I appreciate you getting to know one another, I fear we should not take the risk of discovery by any further delay."

Mariam immediately responded, "Of course. I lost my focus for a moment. Please, everyone, follow me. Tavit and Arexi, I have your bundles safely stored."

The sweet woman turned down a hallway, and everyone dutifully followed her lead. Almost immediately, she paused by a cluster of mops, brooms, and pails. She cleared them away, revealing a trap door. Now, she stepped back and allowed Tavit to lift the door, leaning it on the wall behind the opening.

"Ah-hah!" The sight of the door caught young Hrant's attention at once. This home had a secret trap door like the one he had found in their stable. His hope for a safe escape was firmly bolstered. At the same time, Hrant realized they were not near home.

After Tavit descended the ladder, he lit a torch on the wall nearby and called up to the others. "Yes, our bundles are indeed right here. Please pass the Gulumian family's goods to me."

Aghavni and Arexi handed the three packs down to Tavit. Then Arexi helped Aghavni, Vahram, and Hrant down the ladder to her brother.

As Arexi descended, everyone offered final words of gratitude and farewell to Mariam, an official gatekeeper. They stood in the dimly lit tunnel and waved to her as she closed the trap door once more. They could hear her placing her cleaning items atop the wood.

Now Tavit turned and headed down the rough corridor, with the others following silently. Arexi brought up the rear.

Hrant could not help but think how different this tunnel was from the one he had been in with his father. This was more narrow and so much more winding.

Finally, after what seemed like half an hour to Hrant, he realized they had by-passed a couple of side corridor intersections. At long last, they emerged into a wider tunnel. He had overheard his mother and Tavit talking, but he did not know that Tavit was leading them to that large stone chamber he had previously seen with his father. Now they emerged in it, and Tavit lit another torch.

"Arexi, please stay with the boys. I am accompanying Aghavni back toward their house. We will not take the chance of going up into her home. However, she has a couple more bundles of valuable food and supplies waiting at their ladder."

Tavit continued with all seriousness. "Please, if for any reason we have not returned within 20 minutes, do NOT wait any longer. Simply go back the way we came and take the first intersection to the right. Follow that without changing course, and you will find the entrance to the resistance hiding area. Someone will help you from that point."

"No, Tavit," Arexi protested. "We will not go without you. I will not hear of it!"

"Yes, dear sister. Yes, you will. You must," stated Tavit firmly. "The chances are that will not be necessary. However, if the Gulumian trap door has been compromised, we may be arrested or killed on sight. Please, promise me. This is so much larger than just you and me now. This is about our people. *All* of our people."

Arexi nodded solemnly. "Yes, Tavit. I promise." Her lips were drawn in a thin tight line, but she knew her brother spoke the truth.

Tavit then explained how unlikely it was that the tunnels had been compromised. Since the tragic assault at the Gulumian home, this section of the Armenian quarters had been especially well guarded.

Only a very select few Turks even dared enter. That included Serkan Raffi with the priests who had come to take care of the bodies of poor Nazeli and Anush. Then the Ottomans seemed to have completely left the neighborhood. Many armed members of the Armenian resistance now gathered there.

Further, there were plans in the works for the trap door in their stable to be removed that very day. The men planned to also repair the floor, leaving no sign of the door to the tunnel. They had also posted a watcher by the Gulumian house. Tavit was sure that he would have been alerted had the Turks been near the house never mind made any such discovery.

Beyond this, he assured the group that if the trap door had been discovered, they most assuredly would have been greeted by a great many Turkish soldiers in this very room. He made all good points.

As Aghavni and Tavit disappeared down the tunnel, Arexi and the boys sat down on the floor along one wall. The boys were still dressed as girls. She smiled at them. "Boys," she started. "While we are underground, you no longer need to dress as girls. But we must save the skirts and shawls. You will likely need the disguises again once we find a safe window for your escape. It would do you no good to have gotten this far only to have the soldiers discover Armenian boys have escaped. They may let little girls live, unscathed. But boys have not been so lucky. The Turks will not risk having you grow up to seek revenge."

The boys' eyes grew wide listening to her, but they were delighted to rid themselves of the skirts and shawls, even if only for a time. To carry less in their bundles, they had worn their trousers beneath their petticoats. Now Vahram and Hrant could not help but wonder if life would ever return to normal again.

Thankfully, in just a few short minutes, Tavit and Aghavni returned with the additional supplies. Tavit extinguished the extra torch he had lit for his sister and the children and placed it in a bracket on the wall. Then he led them back the way they had come.

Hrant found himself wishing they had gone the other way that led up the many steps. It was almost as if he thought that if they had gone up to the top, he might have found Papa. Hrant knew that was not possible; it was just his mind dreaming for a moment.

Still, he loved the image of his precious home and city from high up on the ledge on the side of the rock. He longed to hear his father's voice. Hrant loved his way of explaining life and time. He reveled at how deep and soulful his Papa's dark gray eyes appeared. He enjoyed the careful, measured manner with which his father spoke, especially when topics turned serious. Hrant missed his Papa.

They rushed onward. No time for thoughts of yesterday. No time to be a child.

The Underground Resistance
23

LIVING UNDERGROUND HAD become a way of life for an increasing number of Armenians. Anyone suspected of stirring sentiments against Turkish oppression became an outlaw. Dozens of young men were slated for prison or execution.

If they could reach the literal underground resistance, they found hope. As fighting broke out in Van, the Ottoman military would be surprised to find a good number of young men in the trenches along with the elderly, the women, and the children left in the walled city.

Deep, hidden caves served not only as a refuge but also became central to building a force to stand up against Ottoman aggression. Many men now lived here.

In truth, these caves did not seem to house the criminals Hrant had been warned against as a youngster. At least, bad people did not seem to be here any longer. Then again, the lad realized that these men, part of the underground resistance, were now all likely to be considered criminals, at least in the eyes of the Ottoman authorities.

He learned that many young men who had escaped from military labor battalions now gathered here. Also, as it turned out, many young men had opted to come here directly, instead of joining the Ottoman Army when those orders had arrived.

Thankfully, freshwater springs and irrigation canals abounded in the caves under the Van Castle. Supporters and sympathizers secretly delivered other supplies, along with news from the outside world.

Garabed had hinted at the extent of this underground system to his wife, but Aghavni was still caught unprepared for what they were now seeing first-hand.

Tavit led them past several men sitting on the cold stone floors of the cave. They all held weapons, though no imminent danger seemed apparent. Others had already taken their places in the trenches that continued being dug.

Indeed, various little streams of fresh, naturally cool water flowed from the springs and in canals from deep inside the Varek Mountains. That was life-sustaining for these men. However, it was evident there was no great abundance of food. The atmosphere was very dark, but it felt comfortably cool to the skin.

While they walked, Tavit pointed to a small alcove on the right. "This is where you and your family will stay. This is just a brief stop for you. But, before you start your journey, you will get rested. Then Arexi will travel with you to Russia."

"No, Tavit," Arexi protested immediately. "I will not go to safety without you. Each other. That is all we have left. There is plenty I can do here. I can prepare food. I can care for the sick and wounded. I can shoot a rifle. You know that I am a very good shot. You told me I am like a fine marksman."

Tavit scrunched up his mouth into a grimace. He did not want his sister in danger. And yet, if he was being honest with himself, he had not been relishing the moment when they would be separated. She was right that they could certainly use her help. He feared that once the serious fighting began, they would likely need her much more than even she realized.

"All right," he gently said, slowly nodding his head in acquiescence. "But you must agree to follow *my* instructions and leadership."

Arexi nodded without hesitation. "Ready to serve, as assigned, dear brother."

Now Tavit continued his brief tour of this section of the hidden caves. He gestured toward an opening on their left.

"Though humble, this is our infirmary, of sorts," he began explaining. "We are prepared for six patients, but as of now, young Toros Kherbekian is our only guest."

"What?!?" Aghavni exclaimed. "Toros? Toros Kherbekian?"

"Yes," replied Tavit. "He has spent two weeks in and out of consciousness, and he has only ever uttered one word. Nazeli."

Aghavni gasped. Hrant did not hesitate. He broke away from his mother and rushed through the small opening into the side chamber. The lone figure on one of the six beds was easy to spot, even in the lantern's dim light.

"Toros! Toros! Toros!" Hrant cried out.

Dropping to his knees at the bedside, he grasped the dangling hand of Toros. His would-be brother was alive! Now the entire group had entered the infirmary. "How do you possibly know Toros?" Tavit was utterly caught by surprise.

Aghavni reached out and took Toros' other hand in hers. Her voice grew soft.

"Nazeli is my daughter who was engaged to marry Toros when he returned from the front. My daughter... one of my daughters who was just murdered." Aghavni dropped her head as tears now ran down her cheeks unabashedly.

Oh, my! Both Tavit and Arexi stared at each other wide-eyed. Arexi immediately wrapped her arms around Aghavni and simply held her as the older woman's body shook with grief. She trembled, but not quite uncontrollably. Yet, she shook. Her stomach and chest heaved. She allowed the pain to surface in a manner she had not permitted herself to feel when the horrifying acts had taken place that stole her daughters from her. Now she openly, wretchedly, and visibly ached.

Aghavni somehow maintained a slight sliver of control, however. She did not permit herself to cry out loud. Wailing would assuredly echo throughout the caves, and she instinctively sensed the danger should her cries reach enemy ears. The grieving woman somehow managed to squelch what she was sure would come out as cave-rattling sobs and cries.

Meanwhile, both boys were clinging to the bedside of the very still Toros. He had not stirred even the slightest bit, despite all that was going on around him.

Tavit now joined the little family and began sharing what had been learned about this precious patient in their cave. Everyone listened intently.

"We were told that Toros had been taken to a field with all the other young men in his Armenian regiment. Their weapons were then confiscated by the Turkish. Sadly, this appears to have become the standard practice. Naturally, he and the others believed they were being sent to a labor detail, as this, too, was happening with growing frequency.

"Please remember, dear family, that Armenians have increasingly become excellent marksmen, also. This gives the Turks yet another reason to not trust us. Nor do they dare stand shoulder to shoulder with us in battles. They recognize that we may be sympathetic to the Russian Empire, as the Russians have often offered us assistance.

"All the pontificating on politics matters little. This day brought no hard labor, never mind comfort for your beloved Toros.

"In fact, the Turks opened fire, using the Armenians' weapons against the now unarmed young men. The shooting continued until all the Armenians had fallen.

"Sometime later, Toros awoke to find two comrades dead on top of him. Toros' wounds were severe, but he was alive, although just barely.

"Under the cover of darkness, and amidst all the blood and pain, he was able to wriggle free and drag himself out from under the pile. Toros then found one other Armenian lad who had also survived.

"Toros helped pull him out, and, together, they secretly made their way to the dock in Bitlis. They avoided Ottoman military personnel and found dock workers. Their fellow Armenians successfully smuggled them back across Lake Van... home and to the safety of our secret tunnels.

"The other young man recovered quickly. We located his family, and our resistance forces helped them all escape. They headed over the mountains to Yerevan. Before leaving, he shared with us all the details I have just told you.

"I am sorry to say that Toros has not been so lucky. His wounds were far worse. One bullet had passed close to his lungs.

"He has only regained consciousness a couple of times. And, as I mentioned, the only word he has uttered turns out to be your daughter's name... Nazeli."

Now, as if having heard the name of his beloved spoken, Toros began to stir. Everyone turned to him.

Hrant spoke first. "Toros! Toros! It is me, Hrant. Can you hear me?"

Without opening an eye, Toros spoke as if in a dream. "Hrant! Dear little Hrant! What on earth are you doing here? You are too young to get caught up in this mess."

Aghavni spoke next. "Toros, just rest now. We will all talk later."

Upon hearing her voice, Toros opened his eyes. He was not dreaming after all. What was going on?

His eyes glanced rapidly around the dimly lit small space and at the little group standing around him. Ever so slowly, he started remembering what had happened in that miserable meadow. His fellow Armenian soldiers. The Turkish soldiers lining them up and then shooting them all. Crawling out after dark and finding their way to the harbor. But how did Nazeli's family find him?

Nazeli! Oh, yes! Now Toros became fully awake and started to try to sit up.

Wincing with pain, he slumped back down again, but he called out, "Nazeli! Where are you, my beloved?"

"Oh, dearest Toros," Aghavni began. "You are all she ever thought of or talked about all day and night. Believe me, she would be here if she could choose to be anywhere."

She clasped his hand between both of her own, the crushed one of which had been cleaned and bandaged by Arexi. Aghavni struggled to find the words to say. She repeated herself as she shared.

"Please know that we all wish dear Nazeli was here, and she truly should have been. But sadly, I regret to share with you, that we have all lost her forever. Nazeli… is gone, Toros."

"No! This is not possible," Toros could barely utter the words. He pinched his eyes shut. He knew she had not been ill. She did not lead any sort of dangerous life.

"In the name of God, what happened?" These were the only words poor Toros could squeak out.

Aghavni slowly sat on the edge of the bed beside Toros before answering. She shook her head, as though trying to make some semblance of sense of it all, even for herself.

"Toros, we knew dangerous times were coming, but they have arrived. Soldiers ambushed my husband and his relief party as they were heading home. They killed Garabed and his father. As if that is not sad enough, they were not done.

"They then came to our home, where they shot both Nazeli and Anush. We three, Vahram, Hrant, and I, are all that remain of the Gulumian family in Van. We were ordered to leave. The soldiers had us, almost marched us out of the city, but we escaped. Arexi and her brother, Tavit, rescued us."

Toros now struggled to prop himself up a bit higher in the bed so he could look in Aghavni's eyes more directly. He winced, but no one could be sure if the pain stemmed more from his injuries or this latest tragic news. Arexi quickly moved to prop a pillow behind him for support.

He started to speak now. Thoughts, words, images all flowed from Toros, despite his weakened condition.

"These Ottomans, they have carved out my heart. They cut us, our families, to the core. They attack. Maim. Slaughter. Yet, they feel no remorse. They have no respect. They laugh! They will never be satisfied until not one of us remains. They intend to annihilate us all!"

Toros was angry and wounded. In his heart at this moment, he felt little mercy for the Ottoman Empire.

Everyone, even Vahram and young Hrant understood. They all felt great torment and confusion, along with heartbreak and deep mourning. Tears flowed down both boys' cheeks. They, too, had not been permitted even a moment to grieve.

Toros softened his tone as he continued. "With or without my beloved Nazeli, you are still family to me. If you will have me, of course. As you know, my sister and mother left long ago. You and your family are all I have left here, too. No matter what happens, you will always and forever remain my beloved family."

His voice cracked as his anger slipped into grief. Tears fully welled in his eyes. Little Hrant reached up and brushed away a tear that rolled down Toros' cheek. The lad then revealed great insight for such a young boy.

From the Mouths of Babes

24

HRANT SPOKE SOFTLY. "Toros, I loved my sisters, too. And my Papa, and my Grampa. I still love them. We will always love them. We will also always love you. You have already become another brother. I am sad we will not have a wedding for you and Nazeli, but you are family now anyway. There is nothing the bad soldiers can do to change that."

Toros reached up and took Hrant's hand in his own. He nodded. He did dearly love this little lad.

The young boy continued, "We are all very, very, very sad right now, Toros. But while the soldiers take away the people we love, they cannot take away our love, our memories, all that we have shared and meant to one another.

"This is hard for me to believe some days, but I try to remember what Papa said. He told me we need to remember that just because the Ottomans do evil *things* does not mean they are evil *people*. They are what Papa called 'misguided.' When *they* behave badly, *we* need to work much harder to not behave badly, too. That would be even *more* horrible because we know their behavior is just plain wrong.

"We love you, Toros. You will always have our love. They cannot take that away. No one can take that away. I do not care how many guns or how much hatred they have. Love is stronger. *Our* love is stronger. It has to be."

The atmosphere in the room had been lilting deftly.... reflecting wild swings from anger and pain to mourning and utter weariness. Hearing the youngest Gulumian child speak so calmly brought desperately needed peace and fortitude to everyone's hearts.

Aghavni wrapped her arms around Hrant. She kissed him lightly on his head.

"Thank you, sweet child," she said. "You are your father's sage son." No other words seemed needed.

A calm sort of silence hovered in the room for what may have been far more than a few seconds. No one seemed to want to snap back into reality.

Tavit knew they could not just stand still, despite the dire circumstances. Or perhaps because of the dire circumstances.

"Toros," he started. "According to the doctor, you need to stay in bed for a few more weeks. Unfortunately, we need to help the Gulumians begin their trek toward Russia... now. Time has become a challenge.

"You would not be aware of this, but there are growing numbers of cannons poised outside the walls of our city. As you well know, the military has already taken all able-bodied Armenian men out of the city. We are many who would not go. All of us. There are many young men here... underground. There are also many older men in the city. Young and old... we will not leave. That would leave Van totally at their mercy, and we know the Ottomans have no mercy.

"We are sorry to tell you this, Toros, but we surely face battle within just hours. You will not be able to join us, at least not in these first days as we defend our city. But right now, we must prepare what remains of your little family to begin their journey in the morning, if at all possible."

"We cannot leave Toros behind," Aghavni stated firmly. "We all have prayed for so long to find him, and now that we have, we should stay together."

"No," Toros protested immediately. "That is not a choice you can make at this point. This is not a place that is safe for a mother and two young sons.

"Aghavni, your husband used to teach me many wise things. One I always remember is that the clouds that thunder do not always bring rain. However, he also warned that in this case, in these times, we are in the direct path of a tremendous and dangerous storm."

"He is right, Aghavni," Tavit agreed. "You must do all you can to get to safety. These caves will become overridden with soldiers. We will fight to protect our city and our homes. Your job is to get to Russia, per Garabed's plan for you. You must protect these two boys. They are Garabed's youngest sons. They must grow up to breathe the air of freedom."

"How long do you think it will be before we can return?" Aghavni was deeply rooted and sorely wished they did not have to depart.

"Only God knows that answer," Tavit stated simply. "The Russian soldiers are coming to our aid. With their help, we will succeed in holding our city. Will that be for long enough for the Young Turks to give up their total plan to remove or eliminate Armenians? We do not know.

"But you can be sure that we will be communicating as best we can to get word to both Yerevan and our contacts over the border in Kars, Russia. You will be able to learn of our progress... or of our demise. Please assure us that we can count on you to persevere. No matter what happens to us or our dear city, we will be doing what we must do.

"Helping families escape to safety gives us hope that we Armenians will ultimately persist, despite the Ottomans' most dire efforts to thwart us. We need your assurance that you will do all that *you* can to help these two boys stay alive, grow up, and remember. *That* gives us strength and renewed purpose."

Aghavni looked at her two wide-eyed boys. She knew Tavit and Toros were right.

"Of course," she began. She turned to Tavit and Toros. "We will all do our best to get to Russia. If we succeed, we will wait in Kars. And while we pray every day and every hour for your success here and for a rapid end to these times of trouble, we will remember. We will never forget what the Ottomans have done to us. We will never forget the bravery and courage of you and so many other Armenians to stand up to the monsters, even though the monsters are far larger and better armed than we. We will never forget Garabed, Ohanes..."

Aghavni's voice cracked. She paused, swallowed hard, and pressed her eyes shut as she continued. "...dear Nazeli, Anush, and all the other loved ones martyred in these beastly days."

Arexi spoke up now. "Aghavni, we will look after Toros. I will make sure he gets well and fully recovers his strength. Please trust me. Please. Remember, a friend is necessary in difficult days. These are truly among the most difficult days. God willing, we will all meet again... soon. We will, eventually, be able to get word to you in Kars."

Aghavni opened her eyes and looked at the sweet Arexi. How full of gratitude she felt that the young woman had risked her own life and her own family's safety to take in this trio of strangers from the terror of that hideous, dark alley. How blessed she felt now that Arexi would stay behind and care for their beloved Toros and any other Armenians needing care.

"Yes," she finally said. "We each have our jobs to do, don't we? We will do them and honor our dear loved ones and *all* our fellow Armenians."

"Mama," little Hrant said. Before continuing, he straightened himself up, standing as tall as his young frame would possibly allow. "We can do this. Papa said that we must persist. Vahram and I will be strong. We all will succeed. You... will... see."

"Ah, my wise babies." Aghavni managed a slight smile. "Your Papa has taught you well. Another of his favorite proverbs noted that there is a life of iron and a life of silver. Today we are in the life of iron. We must be strong.

"We must not lose faith. We will persist, so we can savor the days of sparkling silver that lie ahead and remember those shining memories of our yesterdays. Today? Ours is a life of iron."

"Iron, Mama," Hrant said. "We can do it." He turned to his brother.

Vahram echoed. "Iron, Mama. We *will* do this."

Aghavni reached out and took ahold of both boys' extended hands. "We go forward. We will bring honor to our family and our people. Thank you, boys."

She gratefully looked at Arexi, then Tavit, and finally at Toros. "Our deepest gratitude to all of you. May God bless all our steps."

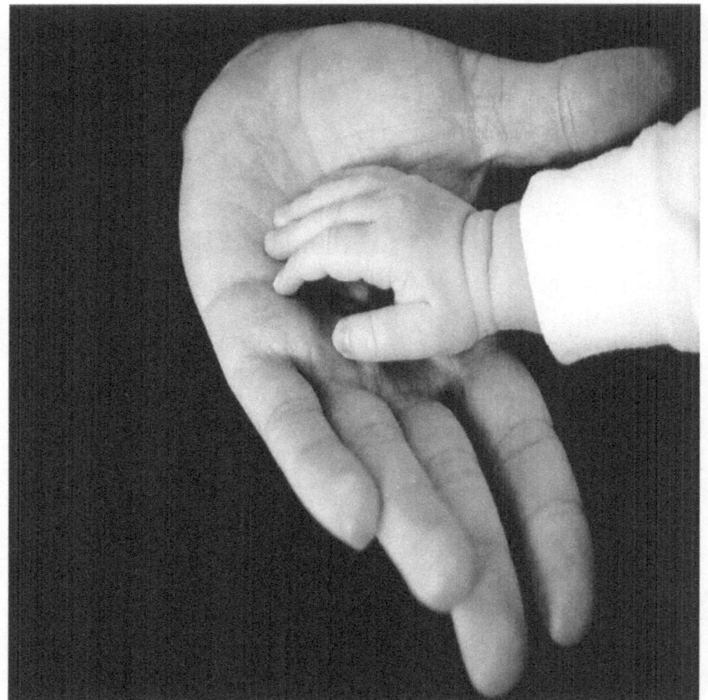

Photo courtesy of Liane Metzler

Escape to Ararat
25

BEFORE DAWN, THE little family said its final farewells to Toros, Tavit, and Arexi. Aghavni looked at them all, truly wondering if they would ever lay eyes on each other again. She could not think of that now.

With scant parcels of food and meager skins of water, they would ration their supplies during the long days ahead. The small amount of fried lamb Aghavni had packed in their sacks would simply have to do, as it was the only meat that could travel safely. They would not have the means to cook anything. The bread, cheese, nuts, and dried fruits would serve them well. Water was her deepest concern.

Dressed as little girls again, with their small packs on their backs, Aghavni took the hands of her brave children and stepped into the darkness of the fading night. They needed to be well clear of the city when the first rays of dawn appeared.

They would avoid the deep snows and highest peaks, of course. They would also have to avoid main roads and the towns along the way. They could meander along some of the lesser riverbanks for a time, but there would be few if any, paths to follow once they left the plateau and began to climb the mountains.

Further, Tavit has warned them not to trust taking sanctuary in any monasteries along their route. Rumors had surfaced of some of their own clergy reporting to the Ottomans about Armenian survival efforts. Somehow, it appeared, these men thought that their treachery would buy them some sort of saving grace with the Ottoman Turks.

Tavit thought them utterly foolish to still trust leaders who lied with such ease. And he found it utterly disgusting that they were committing these acts of broken trust against their fellow Christians. Such were the times.

Decades later, when Hrant's wife wrote her journal memoir for their grandchildren, she commented on the little family's escape. Again, Marjorie was not an Armenian by birth. However, she had grown to feel the heart and soul of these challenged people.

She became Armenian by marriage, but, more specifically, she became what one might call an Armenian by choice. One choice she made was chronicling Hrant's story to help the next generations never forget.

"They ended up running for their lives. He was just nine years old. His brother was somewhat older. They knew they were lucky to be alive, but they feared they'd be discovered at any moment and be killed. Grampa told me that he had no feeling of embarrassment as they walked along, dressed as little girls. There was only terror, bloody bodies, and the smell of death. They just kept walking, quietly, rapidly.

"As an adult, I've heard the stories of the rivers that 'ran red with blood.' I understand. Grampa talked about having to silently walk past the butchered bodies of his friends. The Turks had either left the bodies where they fell or tossed them in the rivers.

"Hundreds of bodies. Thousands of bodies. There had been no regard for decency or human life.

"Without adequate food and water, my family... your family... had, instead, walked over Mount Ararat to escape to Russia. Walking to Europe, while slow and painstaking, proved to be the right choice. At the time that they ran, the Turks had not wanted any of the Armenians leaving the city of Van.

"I suppose it wouldn't have helped them do their evil deeds had word of their massacres leaked outside the Ottoman Empire. Of course, as families, such as the Gulumians and others escaped, action got stepped up by the Turks to put stricter controls on the Armenians. They had already taken all the able-bodied men up to the age of forty. They had mostly then been killed.

"Next, they began rounding up the elderly, the women, and the surviving children. Many young women were taken prisoner for Turkish harems.

"Those that resisted and fought back were raped and murdered. Others, as Turkish troops approached, would throw themselves in the lake or the rivers to drown rather than be taken prisoner by the Turks."

"Children," Aghavni quietly ordered the boys. "Just keep your eyes facing forward."

She had recognized the bodies of neighborhood families they passed. She knew Vahram and Hrant were seeing the bodies of some of their friends. She could only assume that they also recognized the agony on the faces of people they knew so well.

And there seemed to be no end to the death around them. How on earth could one people be so brutally cruel to another people? How could they not recognize Armenians as people? Christians are people. Families are people.

What possessed the Turks to think they had any right to simply disregard, never mind eliminate people who believe differently than they do? This was simply barbaric.

If they could survive this journey, Aghavni recognized it would take more faith than she was certain she had to find even a smidgeon of forgiveness for all the hatred and lack of mercy they were witnessing.

She reminded the boys again, "Keep your faces tilted downward." She hurried them along, mindfully aware of several other small groups of people doing exactly what they were doing. So many people were trying to escape with their lives. Yes, they were avoiding the main road, but so were many others.

When she heard a shot ring out, Aghavni immediately ducked her head and pulled the boys behind some nearby rocks. Ordering them to keep their heads down, she slowly peered around the rocks to ascertain the current situation.

They had initially circumvented the village of Karahan and were now a great distance past the Monastery. As they drew well into the wilds by this point, Kurdish bandits loomed as a growing danger.

The Ottoman government was paying them well to rain havoc, death, and destruction down on the Armenians at every possible opportunity. Hazards lurked at every corner.

Now the threatened danger had reared its ugly head. Vultures circled ominously overhead. Aghavni did not want their bodies to become a future meal for the scrawny scavengers.

She felt for the gun under the layers of her garments. She was as ready as she could be. Interestingly, she observed that her hand was not trembling even the slightest bit.

She felt her lips tighten. At the same time, she recognized that the prospect of shooting someone who may be trying to kill them did not make her nervous after all.

From their hiding place, Aghavni could see at least half a dozen bandits herding two small family groups together. They shouted at the families to surrender all their goods.

The families were pleading for mercy. Pleading for the bandits to spare them or at least to spare their children. The adults seemed fully aware that they would not be getting out of this dire situation alive.

The Gulumian trio could do nothing to help. There was no time for hesitation. Nor was there room for guilt in trying to save themselves, while leaving these poor people to their fates. She also knew her little handgun would be no match against the bandits' firepower.

She had but the one pistol, because she had given her second one to Arexi before they left the underground. Aghavni knew she could only handle one weapon, and the resistance needed every possible gun for the fighting already underway.

Regardless, Aghavni also recognized she must take full advantage of the current noise and confusion and act immediately, or else she put their lives at an even greater risk.

She firmly took ahold of her sons' hands and quietly, but quickly, began to run in the opposite direction. The sound of the yelling faded as they put more distance between themselves and the bandits.

Suddenly, gunshots sounded far closer than they probably were. Pure terror surged through Aghavni's veins. She knew the bandits were now slaughtering the family.

They did not look back. They did not turn back. They continued climbing.

Each time that little Vahram's weak body seemed to be giving out, she found them a temporary shelter of shrubs or trees. Though they dared not stop for very long, especially during daylight hours, they rested until Vahram's breathing returned to typical or nearly normal.

The fried meat they had packed was nearly gone, but they would share a small sip of water and a crust of bread and some dried fruit for a meal. Then, they moved onward, slowly picking their way up the lower ridges of their sacred Mount Ararat.

Hrant found himself reflecting on stories that his father had shared with him. Mount Ararat was a symbol of their Armenian culture, but Papa had also shared that even back in ancient mythology, their holy mountain was also revered. Their distant ancestors believed Mount Ararat, formed by volcanoes, and looming nearly 17,000 feet about sea level, was the home of their gods.

As they purposefully walked, his creative mind recalled some of the old tales. This helped him pass the time and avoid thinking about the current dangers and all the heinousness they had witnessed.

Now, finally, after several days of uneventful travel, hope glimmered that they just might make this trek to Russia without further incident. Their experience of relative peacefulness was not being shared elsewhere.

During rest stops, they had sadly looked back over the plateau behind them. Their beloved city was under attack. The cannon fire remained clearly audible. And seemingly ceaseless. Smoke billowed wildly. They said their prayers.

While the nights had been very cold, the family now found themselves wrapping up in their blankets even during the days. Though they had not even considered going over the snow-capped peak, they frequently found themselves amidst small patches of snow, lingering even into Spring.

They took refreshment by scooping up handfuls of snow and refilling their water skins. Days and nights grew longer, and their supplies grew sparse.

As they were heading down the north slope of Ararat now, they knew these most recent snows would be the last. From this point forward they would rely on freshwater springs.

Though only rarely had they recently seen other Armenians doing exactly what they were doing, no efforts were made to join up with each other. Everyone seemed keenly aware that greater numbers also meant greater chances of being caught. At the most, Aghavni nodded a sign of support to fellow travelers.

Meanwhile, Aghavni, Vahram, and Hrant moved along with hushed, if any, conversation. All efforts were made to remain as invisible as possible.

This gave the trio an abundance of personal time to ponder. To think. To wonder. Hrant could not stop himself from thinking and imagining. Despite the chaos that enveloped them all, or perhaps because of it, he found his mind wandering yet again.

Just imagine. They might very well discover Noah's Ark. His teachers and priests had often referenced the famous story from the Bible. He knew that following the great flood, the Ark had come to rest somewhere on their sacred Mount Ararat.

Could they possibly be lucky enough to catch a glimpse? Likely, it was much further up the snowy peak, but Hrant had silently vowed to keep his eyes open just in case. And he had been doing exactly that for several days. Having such thoughts to occupy his mind proved to be a blessing.

Thankfully, because the trek over the mountain was so difficult, Aghavni had also let the boys remove their skirts and shawls several days ago. Trousers gave the boys far greater ease and agility. She understood. The boys were not accustomed to skirts.

She also had freed herself from the Turkish requirement of a head covering and veil. Naturally, she kept the boys' petticoats, as she knew they would need the money and jewelry hidden within those secret pockets to survive in Russia.

Aghavni understood that disguises, mandates, and pretenses no longer held any purpose or weight. If bandits found them, they would not be spared anyway. If Turkish soldiers found them at this point, they would also be killed.

For a moment she envisioned her carefully hidden, precious triple wedding band ending up in some hideous vulture's nest. Aghavni shook off those nasty thoughts, and they walked on... and on... and on.

Over the next couple of days, the family struggled but failed to find any additional water. Sometimes they saw beautiful, bubbling springs and rushed toward them for a life-saving drink, only to discover they bubbled with oil, not water. Arrrrgh!

The arid conditions were getting worse, but they had no choice. They walked onward. They climbed. They stumbled. They shook with the bitter cold.

How could this be? Aghavni prayed. They had come so far, surely God would not allow them to simply perish due to the elements of nature... not this close to their destination.

She admitted feeling utterly defeated at one time. Aghavni felt relentless tears of despair building. She squeezed her eyes shut for a moment and choked back those bitter tears.

She prayed. "God, forgive me, but I am bitter. I am struck down. Papa had said we did not expect to win against the military might of the Turks, but we most sincerely thought a political solution would prevail. Please grant us the strength we need for whatever lies ahead."

In addition to struggling to survive the elements and their lack of provisions, on more than one occasion they hid from different patrols of Ottoman soldiers. In one incident, Aghavni had heard their voices before they came into view. She was able to hide the family in the boulders until the soldiers passed by.

She knew they must be drawing close to the Russian border. Ottoman patrols seemed thicker here than even on the south side of Mount Ararat. The two nations were at war, after all.

So, she realized that patrols would be larger and more fully armed. But seriously! Could they, as mere everyday Armenian citizens, be such a dire threat to the Young Turks!?!

Aghavni scowled as she realized the Ottomans were highly determined to not let Armenians escape to Russia, where they would surely share reports of the true atrocities being committed by the Ottomans. Of course. The Young Turks wished to be viewed as a progressive people, an advanced society.

Political foolishness. That is the best she could think of the Pashas' endeavors.

Just one day later, they had heard screams that sounded as if they were not very far away. Very soon, the screams were followed by silence.

The family had learned that this meant Armenians trying to escape had been discovered, whether it was by soldiers or bandits, Aghavni had no idea. She presumed it was soldiers, however. Even this close to the border, bandits would have simply shot the refugees.

As they drew closer to Russia, it appeared that the soldiers were slaughtering the travelers they discovered by using their sabers. They did not want any nearby

Russian soldiers to overhear them shooting their own citizens. Oh, no.

Aghavni sniffed with disdain. She then carefully hid the boys and warned them to stay very still and very quiet.

"Vahram. Hrant," Aghavni began. "I will try to find out in what direction those soldiers are moving. We are extremely close now to Russia. Do not lose hope. If you hear anything... any disturbance... do NOT come out of hiding. I mean that.

"If I do not make it back here, you wait until a long time has passed. Then you continue along the same course we were going. You will get to Russia. Look for Russian soldiers. They will help you. You have two names of people to seek out in Kars. I will try to get back here, but regardless, remember, we must be strong. Life of iron."

The boys nodded. They watched silently as their mother crept along the craggy landscape in the direction from which they had heard the most recent outcries.

Photo courtesy of Marek Piwnicki

The Final Stretch
26

AGHAVNI'S DISCOVERY BROKE her heart, if anything remained to still break further. Yet again, people had been slaughtered. This time she found two women and two little girls. The women had been brutally savaged. They all had been hacked to death by Turkish sabers.

She said a prayer. Little power of observation was needed to see the direction in which the attackers had gone. Their bloody boot prints trailed easterly over nearby rocks, disappearing into the trees.

There was nothing Aghavni could do for the ill-fated refugees. She covered the bodies as best she could with what remained of their shawls and clothing items. Regardless, she knew that wilderness beasts would come for the spoils of these heinous crimes. She said another prayer and turned to head back to her children.

Walking, she thought about her two young sons and her two oldest sons in America. She had married as a teenager and gave birth to her first child just one year later. Now, at age 44, Aghavni felt she had seen and experienced more than enough evil and heartache for three lifetimes. She renewed her vow to do everything possible to save Vahram and young Hrant.

Helping the boys from hiding, they strengthened their resolve. Aghavni said her next prayer out loud. Then the weary little family continued their journey.

It seemed that on this day they were dodging Ottoman patrols every hour. This, while harrowing, also reassured them that they must be finally closing in on the Russian border. They moved swiftly and quietly from one stand of trees to another. In between, they would stop and listen, just to be sure no soldiers or bandits lurked nearby. Then they would select a thicket a distance ahead. When Mama nodded, they all ran to the next spot to hide for a moment or two.

They also knew that some soldiers had been specifically searching for them, as well as a couple of other specific families. On two different close encounters, they had heard the soldiers calling out for them by name! Gruff voices repeatedly commanded the Gulumians to come out of their hiding places. Why on God's good earth would they be so important to have landed on a specific list of names being sought?

Come out of their hiding places? They did no such thing. Eventually, the Turkish soldiers had moved their search along and away from the family.

Now Aghavni's thoughts shifted to the next steps. They simply had to be at or, at least, near the border. Of course, she had been thinking this for two days.

She did not speak Russian. They all spoke Armenian and Turkish. The boys also spoke Kurdish and some French, although they had never become nearly as fluent as the girls were.

Aghavni smiled as she recalled the girls taking great delight in speaking in French or English, giggling all the while, anytime they wanted to play tricks on their brothers. She would have to remind them to be respectful and speak Armenian in the home.

Suddenly, from not far behind them, voices interrupted her fond recollections. How had she not heard them coming? These voices sounded terribly close. Unfortunately, the family had just entered a small clearing. There was no place to hide. There was no turning back.

Aghavni grabbed the boys' hands firmly. The determined mother hissed, "Run... as fast as you can!"

With that, they all started running straight forward. No one looked back.

They were closing in on the trees on the far side of the meadow when she heard the voices far more clearly. The men had emerged into the same clearing now.

Instantly, the soldiers spied the fleeing family and yelled out a command for them to halt immediately. They did no such thing.

A shot rang out. It missed.

Still, they did not stop. The trio ran with every shred of energy and strength they had left.

Without a sound, four other men suddenly rushed straight out of the woods just in front of them. Shocked, the family stumbled in unison, Aghavni catching the feeble Vahram before he hit the ground.

When she looked up, prepared now to meet their doom, a wave of clarity swept over her. These men directly in front of them were *not* Turkish soldiers. Nor were they Kurdish bandits. They were Russians!

As if by providence, four Russian soldiers were running toward them. One raised his weapon and fired a single shot into the air. The Turkish soldiers directly behind the family stopped in their tracks. The Gulumians did not.

The little family was swept into the protection of the Russian soldiers. In fact, one of the soldiers extended his arm and pulled the trio in behind him.

An extremely angry verbal exchange followed. The Turks demanded the Russians return their citizens to them. They claimed to have been tracking the family to help them because they had become lost. Though Aghavni understood the words being spoken, she never had to say a word in their own defense.

The Russians appeared to be fully aware of the danger the family would be in at the hands of the Ottomans. This was far from the first band of refugees these soldiers had encountered.

While this area was not an active front in the war, it turned out that Russia had dramatically accelerated border patrols to help the poor Armenians who were running for their lives. These were treacherous times, and the Ottoman Empire had sided with Germany. Speaking broken Turkish, the Russian soldiers told the Turks that in these times of war they could simply take the Ottoman Empire soldiers as prisoners because they were wartime enemies.

Seemingly ready for a physical skirmish, the leader of the small contingent of Ottoman soldiers ignored the Russian warning. He repeatedly insisted that the Russians hand over the trio of civilians to them. They reminded the Russians that they had no right to take or hold their Turkish citizens, even in a time of war. Over and over, they repeated their demands that the Russians turn the family over to them as they were Ottoman subjects.

One Russian soldier leaned close to Aghavni and told her, in broken Turkish, to continue walking in the same direction they had been heading. He assured her that they would come to a guard station with more soldiers. They would be safe now.

The family obeyed and began to walk, though hesitantly, toward the woods. They easily heard the end of the argument. The Russians made it unquestionably clear that they *did* not and *would* not take orders from any Turks.

No more shots were fired. Aghavni peeked over her shoulder to see the Ottoman soldiers retreating to their side of the meadow. Muttering, yes, but they were departing. They had given up.

Aghavni and the boys continued walking, but more slowly, allowing the Russians to catch up to them. Immediately, one of the men handed them his military canteen with fresh drinking water. Aghavni let the boys both drink some water before taking a grateful sip herself.

This family had been delivered into the Russian soldiers' care. They would be forever grateful.

"Spasibo. Thank you," Aghavni whispered repeatedly to the soldiers. "Thank you" was one of the only expressions in Russian she could recall.

For now, they were safe. She had not had a moment to even think about what to do next.

Photo courtesy of Rebecca Asry

Russian Reflections
27

*"Let the Armenian people of Turkey
who have suffered for the faith of Christ
receive resurrection for a new free life."*
-- Nicholas Romanov II, 1868-1918
Russian Tsar, 1894-1917

THE SOLDIERS AT the guardhouse warmly cheered the arriving family. The immediate servings of more fresh drinking water and bowls of hot soup were equally relished by the trio, just as the soldiers knew they would be.

Meanwhile, Kasber Nazaryan was summoned. The young Armenian man had emigrated from the Ottoman Empire a year earlier and joined the Russian Empire's army. The Russian Tsar Nicholas II welcomed fleeing Armenians into Russia and the Russian army. Kasber was grateful to be there. Like many other Armenians, he gladly joined the army.

He could serve as an interpreter for this new family, as most of the soldiers were Russian. Kasber had proven to be most valuable in this capacity, as increasing numbers of Armenians started arriving at their outpost.

Thousands of Armenians now lived in Kars. Most had moved there following the Treaty of San Stefano in 1878, which transferred Kars from the Ottoman Empire to the Russians. It became the capital of the region.

Before Kasber arrived, Vahram fell fast asleep in the corner by a warm fireplace. He was utterly exhausted from their trek that had lasted more than two weeks.

But, no, they could not spend the night there at the outpost. However, they were welcomed to stay and rest for a time. Kasber invited Aghavni and Hrant to sit by the fire and rest also. Hrant joined his brother curled up on the floor.

Once they were rested and refreshed, the soldier would escort them to the growing refugee camp in the nearby center of Kars. They had made it to their destination. For now, Kasber would simply sit with them to help answer any questions they may have.

Aghavni had many. Though she was, herself, too exhausted to talk much, she asked Kasber to give her any information he may have heard about their beloved walled city of Van.

As a mere soldier, Kasber lacked technical details. However, he was able to share that the Russian soldiers had arrived there. When they entered the city the Armenian resistance forces had pushed the Ottoman troops back and had already secured the city. While it seemed impossible as they were dramatically outnumbered and ferociously outgunned, the determined Armenians had done it. They had protected their home. The Russians found the resistance fighters singing in the trenches.

Aghavni shut her eyes and smiled. "Thank God," she softly uttered.

Kasber continued, "But the Russian Empire troops arrived just in time. The Armenians had no back-ups, no relief forces. And they were nearly out of ammunition. They told our forces that they feared that they could only have held out for one or two more days at the most."

Regardless, this was good news. Aghavni found herself hoping they would be able to return home sooner rather than later.

"So, perhaps our time here in the refugee camp will be brief," Aghavni said. She sighed, but Kasber squelched those thoughts.

"Even if we continue to hold Van, travel will not become safe again for quite some time." he continued. "Kurdish bandits have become a force to reckon with.

"Plus, you must remember that the Ottomans have entered the Great War on the side of the Germans. Fierce battles now spring up all along the Caucasus Mountains. You may need to remain here for as long as a year. At least until the war has ended."

"Also," Kasber said, "there is more. You may not realize this, but the Ottomans tried to attack Russia. Thousands of Turkish soldiers died in their ill-planned military catastrophe. It is now said that the three Pashas, needing someone else to blame other than themselves, of course, have decreed that their national humiliation of extraordinary proportions was totally the fault of the Armenians. Enver Pasha, the Supreme Commander of the Ottoman armed forces, has vowed that the Armenians will pay.

"Not that Armenians had anything to do with the Turks' horrific losses on the Caucasus front, because they did not! Their military setbacks simply added fuel to the Turkish fire. While the Ottoman Empire stands, the times of trouble are unlikely to subside."

He observed the obvious disappointment on Aghavni's face. He felt sad for the little family, but he did not push further.

The young man had long ago stopped asking Armenians, as they arrived, about their families and personal experiences. The horror of it all was overwhelming. These were people who had not only just been running for their lives after witnessing and, perhaps, experiencing unspeakable atrocities, but they often also lost more loved ones along their escape routes. Usually, these were elderly or especially young family members.

Kasber learned that it was best to merely try and find something encouraging to say to their newest arrivals. It was not difficult for him, as he knew even the refugee situation was far superior to living under the constant scrutiny, backward laws, and vile sword of the Ottomans.

"Life is not bad here, I assure you. While times are difficult right now, you will no longer be persecuted for being a Christian. You will no longer hear shouts that you are 'gavour,' a pagan. Your family will not be charged exorbitant extra taxes for being Armenian. Nor will you be considered a second-class citizen or sub-human. The city has many thousands of Armenian citizens, as well as Russian and Greek, too."

Aghavni nodded. She understood what he was saying. She was simply saddened by all they had lost. To also give up her precious city was difficult, but certainly far from their worst loss of late.

This was not the first time she had left home, not knowing if she would ever return. As a young woman, she had given up the security of her lifetime home. Her family, the Samargians, had lived in Salmas, further to the southeast than Van.

Nearly a century earlier, many in her city had moved further north or to Yerevan to escape the troubles during the Russo-Prussian War. Her own family had held fast. Salmas was the only home she had ever known.

As years passed, she knew she was promised as a bride for the son of a business associate of her merchant father. Ohanes Argistis Gulumian, a very well-traveled merchant from the Van province in the Ottoman Empire, had strong political ties in Constantinople. He had assured the Samargian family that Garabed, his second-eldest son, was handsome, talented, and kind and would be a worthy husband for their daughter, Aghavni.

He had been right. However, she felt particularly nervous because she had never even met Garabed Ohanes Gulumian, her intended.

The Gulumians came to Salmas for the wedding, hosted by her father. After the ceremony in the cathedral at the St. Thaddeus Monastery and the following celebration, she only had two more days in her precious hometown. She had not realized it then, but that would be the last time she ever saw Salmas.

Aghavni smiled as she recalled how her brother had observed an old Armenian tradition before she left. He had blocked the door, insisting that the groom pay money before he would let Aghavni leave their home.

After some light-hearted negotiating, Garabed gave her brother whatever price he wanted. Then he escaped with his bride.

Thankfully for Aghavni, the area around Van, her new home, appeared strikingly familiar in some wonderful ways. Bold mountains rose from the plateaus. They were even larger than those more familiar to her. And there was the great Lake Van, far larger than the beautiful lake she had known in Salmas.

There were lush, green gardens that were far more lovely than anything she had previously seen. The lands were very fertile, and crops grew abundantly. The people were warm and friendly also. They made her feel especially welcome. Van quickly felt like home to her.

Garabed, now her husband, always called Aghavni his dove. He was steadfastly good to her. As promised, he treated her gently and provided for her and the family very well. He quickly proved to be a man she easily loved and fully trusted.

Later, when his older brother, Argistis, moved from Van to Constantinople, Garabed invited his parents to move in with them. Aghavni had soon grown to love them dearly, too, and she most certainly welcomed the regular female companionship of her mother-in-law.

Losing her during the Hamidian massacres two decades earlier, dealt yet another painful blow to Aghavni. Her own grandfather from back in Salmas perished then also.

While she let her thoughts wander, Kasber explained how rough the facilities were for refugees. There were a few tents, but roofed shelter was almost impossible to obtain.

They would find two tents being used as bathhouses. And one large tent served as an infirmary. There were also stations where local and national support groups regularly handed out food and water. He advised them that often the water in the camp was not the best. If possible, they would want to buy clean water from the merchants, when they could.

Facilities here in Kars were far from as extensive as those in other, larger cities, such as Alexandropol and Etchmiadzin. Aghavni assured him that they were immeasurably grateful to be alive and safe.

The boys had now awakened, and Kasber escorted them all to the refugee area. Aghavni and the boys were utterly unprepared for what they found there.

Photo courtesy of Jonathan Forage

The Camp
28

ROWS OF SHABBY tents loomed as they rounded a corner by a local cathedral and approached the camp. The refugee area had started on the grounds of the cathedral, but it had overflowed into a nearby meadow. Many dozens or perhaps even hundreds of people huddled in groups beside trees and crumbled sections of old walls.

Suddenly, a wave of terror rippled through Aghavni's body. She saw countless mounds on the ground and realized they were people, covered with scant blankets. Having seen so much carnage, her mind immediately leaped to the conclusion that these were dead bodies.

Kasber felt Aghavni's jerk, pulling her boys back. He followed her horrified gaze.

"No, no," he said, immediately recognizing her perception. "These people are just sleeping. They are resting. We do lose people here, but those who are sick are in the infirmary."

Aghavni breathed a sigh of relief. She and the boys continued walking with Kasber.

A volunteer, one of many Armenians helping at the camp, welcomed them and handed them each some supplies. Kasber said that he would be returning to his barracks then. Aghavni thanked him profusely for his assistance.

As the family walked, Aghavni examined the contents of their little piles of supplies. They had each been given a small, but fresh blanket, a cup, a bowl, and a spoon. Now the volunteer pointed out where the food lines formed each day. She apologized as she explained that it could happen once or twice daily, depending on the delivery of provisions.

"No need to apologize," offered Aghavni. "We are grateful to simply be here and be safe."

They were shown the area used for latrine purposes, along with tents for bathing. There was also a tent for refugee priests, but it varied as to where prayers were being said or services held. And, just in case, the volunteer pointed out the tent that served as an infirmary.

Aghavni recalled learning that several months earlier, the Russian Grand Duchess Tatiana Nikolaevna had established the Tatiana Committee. Through the determined efforts of the daughter of Tsar Nicholas II, financial assistance for refugees had been raised. The committee also was helping with resettlement efforts in Russia, tracking relatives who had become lost or separated, and providing meal stations and hospitals, which they were seeing the results of now.

As evening drew near, Aghavni heard that no space remained available for them in any of the existing refugee tents. More tents were expected in the next few days. Understanding dawned. This explained why she had seen many people sleeping on the open ground.

She thanked the volunteer who helped them settle in beside a wall on some nice grass. She truly felt grateful. After sleeping among rocks and the stress of avoiding wolves, bandits, and Ottoman soldiers, a few more nights sleeping on the ground in a safe environment shone as a welcome improvement. Plus, there would be food, regardless of how meager.

As Aghavni spread her largest shawl out on the grass, she explained to the boys. "This shawl will be our floor. Our room. It is our home for now. We can pretend we are sleeping on the roof at the summer house. You boys will sleep closest to the wall, and I will sleep here on the outside.

"Is this wonderful? We have three new blankets. Best of all, we will sleep tonight with no fear of gunfire or swords or soldiers or bandits or fierce brown bears or other wild animals attacking us."

The boys nodded, but Hrant seemed unsure. "Will we really be safe here in Russia, Mama?"

"Oh, yes," replied Aghavni without hesitation. "The Russians protect Christians. They were not prepared for there to be so many of us, but is it not a blessing that hundreds of Armenians have already safely arrived here?"

Now both boys nodded, enthusiastically agreeing with her. She continued.

"This city called Kars is a place your Papa selected. Almost half the people living here are Armenians. Papa had a good friend here. Tomorrow we will set about finding him and the proper people who can help us contact Aram and Ohan in the United States. We must get word to them about all that has happened and that we are safely in Russia. For now, dear children, say your prayers and bundle up as best you can. We will huddle together and sleep warmly and peacefully tonight."

As they settled in, Aghavni kept a positive expression on her face. She displayed a hopeful spirit, but she had serious doubts inside.

So much had happened. Her sons in America surely were worrying madly. Aghavni had much heartache to share with them. For now, she needed to focus on caring for the younger sons. Though her elder daughters' petticoats were lost, they still had many coins and jewelry pieces. Yet, she had no idea if they could find fair merchants who would trade with her. Well, she would not think about that now.

As she drifted off to sleep beside her slumbering boys, Aghavni pondered the proverb often repeated by her dear husband, as he encouraged them to save any extra money they made. "Silver money is to be kept for dark days." Dark days were clearly behind them and, possibly, ahead of them, too.

Life as Refugees
29

AT THE TELEGRAPH office and with the help of Garabed's merchant friend in Kars, Aghavni got a great deal of information. She also sent her first message to her eldest sons in Boston. It would be delivered to the shoe factory where Ohan worked.

> *Dear Ohanes and Aram (STOP)*
> *Heartbroken to report Turks killed*
> *Papa, Grampa, Nazeli and Anush*
> *(STOP)*
> *Vahram, Hrant, and I are safe in Kars,*
> *Russia (STOP)*
> *Misag is very helpful (STOP)*
> *Awaiting tents in refugee camp*
> *(STOP)*
> *Love, Mama (STOP)*

In mentioning the name "Misag," Aghavni referred to Misag Minassian. He was an Armenian merchant trusted by her husband and father-in-law. He had moved to Russia several years earlier.

As one of the contacts Garabed had previously instructed Aghavni to locate, he could be trusted to trade fairly. He also knew high-ranking Russians, and he had their favor. Perhaps more importantly, his best friend published the city's news and could keep them apprised of everything important that was happening. He would also relay information to and from America and help them send and receive letters.

Over the next days and weeks, Aghavni got to know the lay of the land very well. While they felt safe from Turkish soldiers, there were still dangers and pitfalls in the refugee camp.

She also felt a gnawing and tugging at her heartstrings. It pained her to realize that she now had no way of communicating with anyone back in Van. All services had been cut off in the walled city... or whatever remained of it.

She could not learn what had become of Toros, Arexi, and Tavit or get word to anyone that the Gulumian trio had made it safely to Russia. All she could do was pray for the safety of everyone back in Van.

In hopes that something might change for the better, she left details with everyone's names with Misag and his publisher friend. She was most specific about Toros, Arexi, and Tavit. Aghavni wanted to be certain that if any of their friends or family searched for them there, information would be shared.

She realized it might not happen for weeks or even months. Still, one never knew when somebody might try to locate family and friends down the road. Thankfully, she had also thought to share with Toros their destination in Russia.

Their possessions, few and meager as they were, also fell to a constant risk of being stolen. For fellow Armenian refugees, times were desperate. So, too, some of the people. Even once they were able to be sheltered in a tent, it was amidst several other people.

Sickness also surrounded them. Death gave no holiday. Many who passed away had simply failed to recover from the weariness and trauma of their harried treks to freedom.

Or their weakened bodies were particularly susceptible to every germ and sickness they confronted. Many got sick. Most recovered eventually, but recovery was challenging.

Regular medical treatment was often difficult to come by in the camp, despite the many volunteers' greatest efforts on their behalf. The infirmary tent filled beyond capacity. Sadly, dozens of Armenians seemed to be dying each week.

"Argh!" Aghavni thought. "We have all tolerated so much abuse and hatred. Now, must we finally escape only to perish at the hands of Mother Nature? God's plans are mysterious indeed."

Most of those who took ill fell prey to dysentery. Drinking water at the camp was not the cool, crystal clear water to which their bodies were accustomed from the natural springs and rivers flowing into Van. Like many others in the camp, they had taken fresh, clean water somewhat for granted. It flowed naturally from their mountain. Not so, here in Kars.

Both Aghavni and Vahram became severely ill. Though it was summer, and the days and nights were warm, they both suffered terrible chills and abdominal pain. Nausea and vomiting, along with all-encompassing fatigue left neither of them able to more than barely get out of bed.

Like other ailing Armenians, they had to stay in their tents. The infirmary became restricted to only those people with even more severe ailments.

Because he seemed to be suffering less, young Hrant rose to the challenge of helping them like the trooper he truly was. He spent his mornings standing in lines to get supplies for the family.

One long line started his day before the sun had even arisen. That line was for one small loaf of Russian black bread... *if* he was lucky enough to be among the countless outstretched hands to receive one. Some days, just before he could grasp a loaf, the baskets were empty, and the doors slammed shut again for the day. On many days, he succeeded.

"Khleg, spasibo! Bread, thank you," Hrant gleefully called out.

When he scored a loaf, Hrant tucked it under his shirt and rushed back to his mother and brother. He dutifully broke off pieces and encouraged his sick family to eat, even just a little. He constantly tried to get them to drink water, too. Occasionally, he found the luxury of some broth to soften the bread for them. After they had finished consuming the bread, Hrant began his next duties.

Hrant learned where the best quality water was, so that was always his second stop to replenish their clean water supplies for the day. The good water cost money, so he was grateful that Mama had given him some coins that he had successfully exchanged for Russian kopeks.

Every day, he purchased enough water to fill their three wineskins and a pail for wash water. He then returned to the tent they now called home, along with three other families.

Next Hrant set about purchasing whatever meager provisions he could find each day. Sometimes it was almonds. Another time, he found dried apricots. On a truly lucky day, he found dried meat or a bit of cheese... or even some cracker bread. Now and then he found canned meat, which was good as there was no ice available for refrigeration.

Through Misag, Hrant learned of an Armenian tailor shop. As Aghavni recovered, he told her about the place. Hrant visited and talked at length with the tailor about his mother and their family business. The owner invited her to visit when she felt well enough to do so. He would hire her to work there.

"Yes," thought Hrant. "The Russian Empire is certainly different than the Ottoman Empire. Without even meeting her, this man was considering giving her a job. A job. And she is a woman! This would never have happened in Van." Hrant couldn't help but think that his Papa would have liked it here because he always sputtered that the Ottomans were unfair to women.

The little Gulumian family needed to work to support themselves. The time had come to plan for life beyond the growing tent city. Their coins and jewelry would not last forever.

Hrant knew that he and Vahram were not as skillful at the tailoring craft as they should be, but they could also work when not doing their studies. The tailor had agreed.

Perhaps, just perhaps, fortunes were turning in their favor. Hrant could not help but think that another of Papa's favorite proverbs showed truth here. "Misfortune and fortune are brothers."

Armenian refugee camp
Photo by Armin T. Wegner
Courtesy of Sybil Stevens
and Armenian National Institute, Inc.

Warnings of Revolution
30

SUMMER WAS IN full swing. More refugees arrived daily, some directly from Armenia. Many were being transferred in from other refugee camps that were even more overcrowded than this one. The Red Cross and other charitable groups were stressed to the maximum as they tried their best to help everyone.

Many volunteers actively assisted refugees to find transportation over land and sea. Others worked to help displaced Armenians and Greeks reconnect with loved ones living in Russia and throughout Europe. Often, people sought ways to get to the United States.

The Great War was raging, so all travel was especially risky and filled with dangers for those who attempted it. In truth, after everything they had been through, personal danger from war seemed somehow bizarrely manageable to Armenians.

Aghavni was grateful to the tailor. He paid foolishly minimal wages for the fine work she did, but she was glad to be able to earn something. The money and jewelry they had secretly stowed inside clothing would help them pay for housing and food when they left the camp. They hoped that would be soon.

Those prayers seemed answered when one of the tailor's regular customers invited the family to rent a small room in a boarding house he owned. Timing was perfect, as the coming Autumn air would bring much colder temperatures, especially at night.

The new arrangements worked well. While Aghavni worked full-time for the tailor, the boys worked some hours, too. They also enjoyed the teachers at the local school. Though it seemed odd at first, even the Armenian girls were openly allowed to attend the same classes as the boys.

Vahram and Hrant learned that Russian girls had been offered public education since the late 1700s, thanks to the ruler known as Catherine the Great. And this included classes beyond elementary levels. The boys chalked it up to one more breath of freedom away from the Ottoman Turks.

Hrant truly found himself enjoying Russia. He was learning the language quite easily, although most of his time was spent with his fellow Armenians speaking their native tongue.

Finally, and blessedly, he heard music again. He danced on several evenings, as people gathered in a neighborhood square. The Russians had new, unfamiliar dances, which he loved learning. And everyone seemed to enjoy singing. This helped evenings sparkle with life. And hope.

Aghavni smiled. Her boys were not getting a particularly gleeful youth. She found true pleasure in seeing them start to smile again, even though only occasionally.

Letters were exchanged several times between Aghavni and Ohan in the United States via their friend, Misag. Concerns were growing over both the Great War and a stirring revolution in Russia.

Rumors of food riots in Moscow and other cities reached Kars. Misag's publisher friend confirmed that these events were really happening. These were not just rumors.

Aghavni suggested to Misag that the Armenians might start some gardens or orchards that could help prepare for the future. Misag reminded her that most people still clung to the belief that the entire refugee situation would be resolved sooner rather than later. No one planned on it lasting much longer.

Sadly, through Misag and Ohan, Aghavni also learned there would be no going back to Van. Not now. Not ever. With the help of the Russians, the Armenian resistance had pushed back the Ottoman military forces and, initially, saved the city. Their friend, Aram Manukian, had even been appointed Governor.

However, Russian troops had been pulled away and sent to more important battlefronts serving the Great War. The Turks had taken full advantage and swept over the city once and for all. Their artillery mounted high above the city on the grounds of the old citadel on the great rock had blasted most buildings into complete rubble.

Anyone who had not escaped was slaughtered, herded into a death march, or imprisoned. The latest word informed them that the Ottoman Empire was now destroying their precious walled city. They were tearing down all the buildings and the walls. They would leave no homes, churches, or buildings of any sort.

Further, reports said the Turks wanted to take back Kars. The Russians vowed to protect and keep it.

The Gulumians ached for what they feared had become of Toros, Arexi, and Tavit. Despite this news, Aghavni was glad for their little room and her work in Russia. Conditions had deteriorated substantially in the refugee camp. Hundreds of Armenians were said to be getting ill and dying in all the refugee camps throughout the region. The Gulumians, on the other hand, felt grateful to have been able to leave the camp and assimilate themselves into a life of sorts.

Hrant quickly came to love Russia. He did not mind one bit that they would simply stay living there. However, he did miss Aram. Now he learned that Mama and the elder boys were making plans for them all in the United States.

Dear Mother,

I am drawing ever closer to becoming a real United States citizen. I have worked long and hard for this great honor, and I feel strong pride. People have been very good to us here.

Both Aram and I have registered for the U.S. military. If they need us in this war, we will gladly serve. We would not have fought for the Ottoman Empire, but we will proudly fight on the side of the United States, a truly great nation to its people.

Meanwhile, I am considering buying a farm and some land here, where we can all have a home. This is a place you and the boys will be safe, even if Aram and I get called into military service. As a family, we will make a new life here in this land of many opportunities.

With Papa gone, my dearest Mother, please do not deny me my birthright to care for you and the family. If you agree, I will send passage money and make travel arrangements for you all through Misag.

Naturally, I will proceed according to your wishes. With the growing talk of Russian revolution, I hope you will make your decision very soon.

With deepest respect and love,
Your son,
Ohanes

What would she do? What *could* she do? Her heart was in Armenia. But then again, so was her heartache.

Aghavni looked at her two young boys. They diligently attended to their studies by candlelight on the only table in their rented room. They never once had complained.

What kind of life could they build out of all this trauma? And now, Misag's publisher friend was confirming the Russian political rumblings. A revolution was brewing indeed.

Food supplies were becoming harder and harder to come by. He told her of great crowds of peasants still rioting for food in several cities. His concerns centered on the fact that if they did not get out before a revolution started, the Gulumian family could likely become unable to leave at all. Further shifting sands found the Ottomans still determined to take back Kars.

Perhaps a fresh start in America was the answer. The boys would all be together again. What remained of her family could be reunited.

Yes. She decided. She would do it... for them.

The Journey Begins
31

THE TRAIN RIDE proved to be smelly, crowded, and rough. None of them had ever before been on a train. To get to the station, they first had traveled by cart to Batumi on the Black Sea. Now, much of their new adventure took them along the rails. Destination? Moscow.

Hrant fascinated himself with the passing sights. How splendid to see rivers and mountains flying by, and they did not have to walk!

He also loved the train itself. He could not have cared less that it was smelly and overcrowded. He loved the tracks and the engine and the sights and the sounds. He became fully intrigued with the entire process. This truly counted as a worthy adventure.

Finally, they arrived in Moscow, the great city. Whatever their expectations might have been, the sights they saw surely did not reflect pre-conceived images of the renowned city. Growing food shortages had led to increasing unrest. Food riots that had broken out a year earlier, had only escalated. Looting of storefronts occurred almost daily.

Now, many storefronts remained boarded up... some because their windows had been shattered and others in attempts to protect their stores and goods. Transient, starving peasants littered the streets.

The Great War had triggered many unexpected circumstances. For example, grain and food supplies were diverted to the various battlefronts to feed the troops fighting against the Central Powers. This left little at home for the civilians.

Further, farms had lost most of their workers, as Tsar Nicholas II's government drafted every able-bodied male into military service. So, no one remained on the farms to plant, tend crops, or harvest. A horse shortage existed, as the military also needed every available horse for the Great War efforts.

Aghavni and the boys were not the only ones new to Moscow to be utterly surprised. Other visitors openly gawked also, especially upon seeing women acting as horses, pulling wagons and carts of whatever goods they could manage.

The shortage of grains had led to the Russian black bread being all that was typically available back in their refugee camp. They now learned that this odd bread looked the way it did because bakers used the abundant black beans to help stretch the ever-waning grain supply.

There appeared to be no shortage of alcohol, however. Several times, Aghavni had to instruct the boys to look away from drunk-looking peasants, staggering in the streets, yelling, slurring loudly, and defecating right out in the open.

Aghavni also learned why they were not traveling from Moscow to Petrograd, as had been the original plan. Petrograd was the name given to St. Petersburg in 1914 at the start of the Great War. To emphasize their position, the Russian Empire had not wanted any cities to even sound German. Now, the once-thriving capital city was overrun with prisoners of war, military forces, and refugees.

These refugees were not the Armenians, as along the Caucasus Mountains. These burgeoning throngs of people hailed from various nations and regions that were becoming occupied by German domination throughout Europe.

Travelers needed to avoid Petrograd at all costs. No problem. Ohanes and Misag had taken care to make alternative arrangements for them in advance.

After purchasing a scant piece of black bread to share among them, these new instructions transferred the Gulumian family to another train, which would take them to the port city called Riga. They traveled overnight, and everyone took advantage of the time to rest.

In Riga, they boarded a boat to Stockholm, Sweden, followed by a quick transfer to Copenhagen, Denmark. No time at all would be spent there either, so they were to avoid going into town. Though bordering Germany, Denmark was one of few countries that was managing to maintain a neutral status in the war. Regardless, it seemed best to not plan any stopover. On the other hand, Denmark was known for having wonderful cheese, and it ran a successful canned meat industry.

Aghavni followed the advice they were given and bought up several cans of meat while there. Meat was only seen once a week at the most while in the border refugee town. She knew that though cans were heavy, the food could sustain them for the long journey ahead, as she had no idea what food might be provided on the ship. While at the harbor, she was also able to purchase some butter, cheese, and bread. Simply put, Aghavni, Vahram, and Hrant felt as if they were feasting as they traveled on the ferry to the port town of Kristiansand on the southeast coast of Norway.

All this trekking across Europe was taking its toll on the little family. At the same time, they were intrigued by all the new sights and languages and people. They felt very separated from life, as though these observations and sounds were somehow surreal.

Clearly, they were in a transitional mode. This was far from the norm for Armenians, a people known for not being at all transient for thousands of years.

After eating, the boys shared Mama's lap and napped for most of the voyage. Just a matter of hours later, they stood in Norway.

The elder brothers had traveled to the United States by ship from Petras on the island of Crete just south of the Greek mainland. Sadly, they did not dare send their mother and brothers along this more familiar route. Travel west in Turkey meant leaving the comparative 'safety' of the Armenian provinces... as if there was any semblance of safety to be found anywhere.

Plus, Germans were known to have several of their famed and deadly U-boats around Constantinople alone. The Mediterranean was far too dangerous for passenger travel as the formerly sporadic naval war events increased in frequency.

That was fine. Norway was another of the neutral nations during the Great War. Every attempt was being made to keep the family safe during what were increasingly unsafe times.

From here, they would finally board a much larger passenger ship, which would make a couple stops in Great Britain before finally heading to New York City from the port of Queenstown on the south coast of County Cork, Ireland. This part of the trip was thought to be the riskiest, as Ireland was part of the United Kingdom and a major enemy of Germany. The family did not have to get off the ship in any ports, however, and the Norwegian Shipping company line was said to have a certain level of protection from both sides of the war.

This sort of propaganda may have helped to make passengers and merchants feel safer. However, in truth, German U-boats had already sunk dozens of Norwegian vessels.

Phew. There was simply no time for real rest. Well, what's danger to a family that has witnessed and experienced all that this one had?

The extensive trip already had brought them through two continents and several nations. Aghavni found herself grateful that the boys spoke some French and, at this point, more than just a little Russian.

She was not as adept as they were when it came to learning to speak other languages. She openly recognized that she would have struggled mightily without their additional communication skills.

Surprisingly, she also felt a twinge of remorse in bidding farewell to everyone, both Armenians and Russians, none of whom she had ever known a year earlier. Naturally, everyone vowed to reconnect down the road.

Aghavni was not sure that any of them could or would find each other again. There always seemed to be a sense of sadness that hovered over each of them. "We would only be reminders to each other of the horrors we have survived," she thought to herself.

Since that time, Aghavni had permitted herself to consider a more positive possibility. After so much divisiveness and oppression, she dared to dream.

"Maybe. Just maybe," she thought, "all these survivors could help each other and the coming generations to recall these tragic times as reinforcement of our values. Sometimes we people need great challenges to appreciate the goodness, no, the greatness in Life."

She uttered a prayer. And she asked a question, "Must we Armenians be forced to bear such great quantities of sadness?"

She knew the answer. She had heard it countless times. To those who are given much, much is expected.

And, despite what they seemed destined to endure at the hands of the Turks, she admitted that they had also enjoyed great success despite Ottoman efforts to keep Armenians down in society. Though not wealthy, she had enjoyed a large and beautiful home. They had wonderful children.

Yes, the Ottoman Turks had taken happiness away. They had brutally murdered her husband, his parents, and her two beautiful daughters. She had lost their home. Even their city! Aghavni shook off the negative thoughts. She must not focus there. She must not lose hope. She still felt thoroughly blessed by her four living sons.

She smiled, remembering how she had pleased her eldest son with her decision to come to America. She let him make all the arrangements, as she knew nothing of the outside world.

Aghavni was also thankful that her eldest sons had wired money for the various portions of the trip. She had nearly exhausted both the money and the jewelry they had brought during the escape.

Challenges were not vanquished either. Misag had pulled no punches when he explained the dangers posed by the Great War. The heaviest risk hovered around the United Kingdom and during the Atlantic crossing.

Now, as they gathered their possessions, all of which fit in two small bags she had made at the tailor shop, her youngest son smiled broadly. The boys flourished during this adventure and had hardly turned their faces away from the passing scenery for the several days of their travel.

They walked together toward the harbor. They would spend one night in a rooming house here in Norway before boarding the ship for the final and longest stretch of their trip.

With so many thoughts rushing through their minds, it is a wonder that they got any sleep at all. And yet, before they knew it, the early rays of dawn hastened their journey.

Kristiansand, Norway
Photo courtesy O. Vidal

The Final Harbor

32

THE TRIO STOOD amidst the throngs of people at the harbor. Everyone anxiously waited for the signal to get on board and get underway.

"Hold onto my skirt, boys," Aghavni instructed Vahram and Hrant. "I don't want us getting separated in this crowd."

So many languages were being spoken. A great many people... pushing... shoving... waiting. Neither Aghavni nor her boys had ever been anywhere like this.

Hrant found himself mesmerized again by the vast array of people. Families huddled together, many as wide-eyed as he was at all the bustle and commotion. Some people were merchants. He saw them barking orders at the crew, busily loading large crates aboard the ship.

He watched other businessmen lounging about, smoking cigarettes, and talking amongst themselves. A few men stood by in military uniforms. They did not appear to be on duty, but Hrant imagined that these troops must be transferring to or from some faraway battlefront in the ongoing war.

He enjoyed seeing all these various people. He recalled his father regularly teaching him that watching and listening were always good ways to learn. Hrant reminded himself again how Papa repeatedly taught him to take care when sharing knowledge. He suggested letting people think you were perhaps even ignorant sometimes, when, in truth, you may be very learned on some topic.

Papa had liked sharing that lesson a lot. He had explained that this could be a useful, diplomatic skill someday, even if only to let someone else think they were smarter than you were. So, Hrant observed, and listened, and learned... quietly.

Now he turned his attention back to the massive ship ahead of them. He knew it must hold hundreds of people. He had already been watching men loading cargo on board for a couple of hours.

The family knew the ship would also act as a sort of ferry, making a couple stops in the United Kingdom, including its final one in Ireland, before crossing the Atlantic Ocean. They also understood that because of the dangers caused by the ongoing war that the ship would make fewer stops than it might have under peacetime scenarios.

Hrant then caught his mother looking at him. She smiled. He recalled how she had chuckled when he once asked if the Atlantic Ocean was as big as their Lake Van. Aghavni had assured him that it was far wider. The total trip had lasted four weeks for both his elder brothers, Ohanes and Aram.

Of course, they had to cross the Mediterranean Sea before even reaching the Atlantic Ocean. He liked imagining that their ships may have made stops in various harbors in exotic nations and kingdoms.

Aghavni and the boys had already traveled from Asia to Europe, crossing Russia and Scandinavia. This final leg of the journey would be shorter for them, as they were closer to the North American continent. Hrant understood. He remembered Papa showing him a map back when Aram left for America.

Oh, how deeply Hrant wished Papa was with them now. His heart ached as he felt he somehow now abandoned his father. He missed him terribly.

Hrant also knew that he would miss Russia. It already tugged at his heartstrings. He had made some nice, new friends. His Russian language skills had become quite good. Hrant hoped he would be able to speak more Russian in America, but Mama had told him that people there spoke English.

Mama spoke no English. Neither Hrant nor Vahram spoke more than just a few words in English. Hrant now found himself wishing he had paid more attention when his sisters started learning the language and reading books printed in English.

Ohan had assured them that in his process of preparing to become a citizen, he had learned English quite well. He would help them. Of course, Aram had been polishing his English skills since his arrival and in his college studies, as well.

Hrant figured that he would, naturally, learn English, too. He wondered if English was one of the various foreign languages that he now heard being spoken around him along the docks.

Just then, a group of men he had thought to be business travelers, started yelling. Two of them were punching each other. The crowd drew back as best they could, but there were so many people on the dock that there was no place to go.

Two of the men in military uniforms stepped in to try and stop the fighting. They ended up becoming part of the brawl.

Suddenly, several of the other men who had been standing in the same group turned on the crowd. They each punched someone!

"Nooo!" Hrant wailed as Mama was one of the random victims now dropped to the ground. Under her left eye, her cheek spurted blood. Both Hrant and Vahram, still clinging to her skirt, were on the ground with her, asking if she was alright.

"I am fine. I am fine," Aghavni sputtered. "But those thugs just stole our tickets!"

Hrant stood up and looked around. It had all happened so fast.

As quickly as the disruption had started, it was over. In fact, all the men involved in the ruckus seemed to have magically vanished into thin air.

Members of three other families were being comforted by traveling companions. They had also been struck. Thankfully, no one's injuries appeared to be serious, but their tickets for passage had also been stolen.

The entire fight had been staged. This ruse was used to steal passage onto the ship! Now, what would they do?

Hrant tugged on his mother's sleeve. He pointed to one of the other passengers. It seemed clear that he had also been robbed.

"He is speaking French, Mama," Hrant said. "The man thinks the ship might give them new tickets. Perhaps they would give some to us, too."

Aghavni gathered the boys and their bags and followed in the direction the man and his family were heading. Another couple that had been victimized was already at the little window.

That couple was expounding on their shared plight. The attendant at the ticket window did not seem interested, nor concerned.

Neither Hrant, Vahram, nor Aghavni understood any of the words being spoken. The message from the attendant was clear anyway. He shook his head firmly.

The customer sputtered, but he got out money and gave it to the attendant. He was buying new tickets.

Aghavni knew this was bad news. Nearly everything they had left was already spent to pay for food and shelter during their time in Russia. Plus, their travels to Norway.

Thankfully, Ohanes had wired funds to them to cover the remaining cost of passage to America. She had but one of her gold earrings left. That would certainly not bring enough funds to buy three more tickets.

Of course, she had her wedding ring. Oh, no. She would work any job to get the money they needed, but her precious ring was all that she had left from her beloved Garabed.

As she pondered their situation, the only remaining people ahead of them finished with the attendant. Hrant had followed much of that conversation, as the man primarily spoke in French.

Now, as the French couple turned to head back toward the ship, Hrant spoke up. "Excusez moi. Excuse me, kind sir." Hrant spoke in French, getting the man's attention. "Could you possibly help us? Or, I should say, help our mother?"

The man stopped. He and his wife looked at the sad-looking trio in front of them. This man had also been punched by the thugs, but he was not bleeding.

"You need medical attention, certainly." The man handed Aghavni his handkerchief and politely continued. "Your mother is bleeding. How might I help you, young man?"

"We are not from here," replied Hrant, speaking in his best French. "We have traveled many days from Armenia and Russia. We are going to America to join my brothers. But those bad men stole everything we have. We do not have more money to buy new tickets, and we do not know anyone here. Do you know where we can go for help and to try to contact our family in America?"

"Oh, my child," the man kindly began. "How I wish I was a man of great means. My wife and I would gladly buy more tickets for you. We can give you money for food." The man started taking a little money from his pocket.

"No, kind sir," Hrant raised his hand, palm forward, in protest. "We are not begging. My family works hard, and we do not want your good-hearted charity. We are a family that always helps other people in need. We regularly give food and shelter to poor and wandering people. We, kind sir, are not beggars. We just need to learn where to go right now. If we can contact our family, they will help us get more passage money."

The man smiled and nodded his head. He thought Hrant to be an amazingly mature boy with a great deal of polite confidence.

A loud blast from the ship's horn sounded. The crew now prepared to begin the official boarding process. The man and his wife looked toward the ship. He seemed to know that he had some time to spare.

He turned back to the family and smiled. Hrant observed the man's calm manner and thought that this was likely not the gentleman's first time traveling on the water.

"Come," the man started. "Follow me. There is a Red Cross very near here. They can help your mother with medical attention. They will also know how you can contact your family in America and where you can stay for a few days."

As they gratefully followed the man and his family down the street, Hrant explained to his mother what was happening and where they were going. All she could think about was how very grown-up her youngest son had become. A barely ten-year-old boy had taken charge in a foreign land.

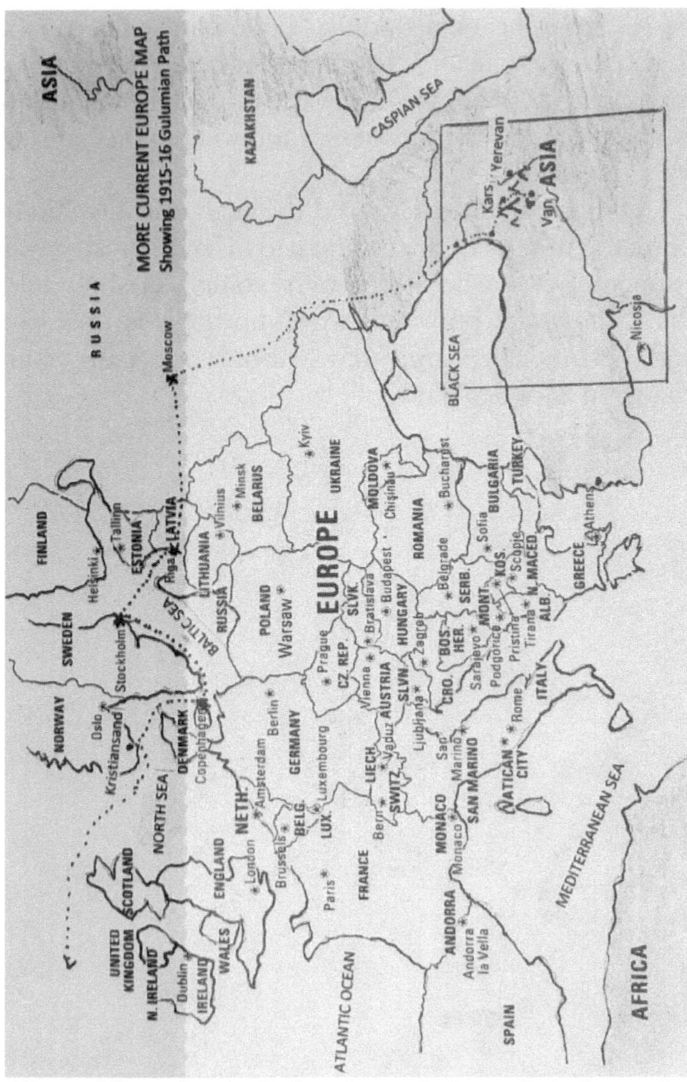

Dotted line shows Gulumian trek from Asia through Europe. Box in lower right corner shows Ottoman Empire's predominantly Armenian area from sketched map enlargement prior to Chapter 18.

Bound for America
33

THE RED CROSS in Kristiansand, Norway patched up Aghavni's bruised face. Their volunteers also fed the family and brought them to a rooming house, where they could share a room for the night at no cost.

The following day, Aghavni found a merchant who agreed to purchase her last gold hoop earring for what seemed a fair price. It was pure gold.

Sigh. She did not mention her precious wedding ring. She feared that if he knew she had anything else of value, the "price" would have included it. That treasure remained securely stitched into the special pocket over her heart. She had not even removed it when she laundered her blouse. Her ring... her sacred ring remained protected.

The money allowed them to stay in the rooming house and eat food for a few days. A Red Cross volunteer also helped them find the United States Consulate office.

Little Hrant served as her translator. They were able to send a telegram to the brothers in America. Again, they had it delivered to the shoe factory in East Boston where Ohanes had now worked for several years. The telegraph office also promised to notify them at the rooming house when they received a reply.

In just a matter of days, details were worked out and money was wired from the United States to finally bring the remaining Gulumians through this final phase of travel to America. Eldest brother John's contacts made short work of gathering the needed replacement funds.

Hurrah! The beleaguered trio was now booked to sail on an even larger ship. The SS Kristianiafjord was also a very new ship, having just been built a few years earlier as the first steamship in the Norwegian-American line's fleet. This beautiful ship had 50 large, private staterooms for wealthy travelers. There were more than 125 additional, though smaller rooms for travelers who could pay the premium price for second-class passage.

These would not be the rooms for this family. They would be among the possible 850 passengers in what was called third class. This merely meant they would be on the lower decks on benched areas in exceptionally large rooms, with shared facilities.

The Gulumians could not have cared less about their travel accommodations. There would be food and light. This new ship even had electric lighting.

Boarding the nearly 1000 passengers onto this wonderful ship was blessedly uneventful. Naturally, being steerage passengers meant standing in long lines, first on the dock and then on a wide metal walkway. They were among those who would embark last.

They struggled with language challenges while checking in, but finally, the officials seemed to understand and got their names, ages, and country of origin, and whatever other information they needed to be written on the ship's manifest. Their paperwork seemed in order. The official inspecting all people boarding finally gestured that the family could proceed up the gangplank to the ship.

Their new route would take them northward over the top of the British Isles. Openly traveling these waters before dark seemed the safest option during these challenging times with German submarines monitoring all traffic on the water.

Three short blasts from the ship's horn signaled their departure. The great steamship lurched as it pulled away from the dock.

Hrant's eyes grew wide as he jumped up and down to catch a glimpse of the shore through the crowd on deck. A great many people stood on the docks. They waved and cheered. Men waved their hats in the air. Shouts of joy and good tidings rang out through the air in a great variety of languages, as the huge ship pulled away to begin its regular route.

This included a couple of additional stops in Norway. Then the huge ship would be crossing the Atlantic Ocean, directly bound for the fabled New York City in a young, but free country.

As celebrations settled down, the trio made its way down the narrow stairs that seemed much more like a ladder. They were, of course, designated to travel in the lower areas on the ship and blocked from even visiting the first- and second-class common areas.

Aghavni and the boys settled into a snug corner amidst the other third-class travelers. They felt most fortunate, having been assigned a very wide, family-sized bunk bed the three of them could share. They saw other families with as many as five and six people all sharing the same-sized bunk.

All three Gulumians seemed to breathe a sigh of relief in unison. The days had been long and filled with stress. What possibilities lay ahead for this small, but determined family? America was widely heralded as the land of opportunity.

No Sultan lauded over them. No Pashas plotted their doom. No soldiers roamed the streets waiting to harass them. No monstrous people would break into their homes and attack them. They would feel safe, if they could finally get there, of course.

Hrant thought of his poor sisters. He knew his mother remained haunted by the fact that the three of them had to run away before seeing to the burials and funeral services for Nazeli and Anush, never mind her husband and father-in-law. Hrant missed them all terribly. It seemed impossible that they were gone forever.

These thoughts could not linger. More dangers lay ahead. The Great War was raging. Even passenger ships faced much peril in the waters around Europe. German U-boats launched torpedoes in seemingly indiscriminating ways. Their ship would not be smuggling anything. They were certainly not a secretly armed military vessel.

Regardless, as passengers, they were told they would be required to wear life jackets for the entire duration of the crossing. This did not offend these travelers. While they prayed that they would be spared by the Germans, they also remembered learning the news just four years earlier of the Titanic, a magnificent ship that sank after hitting a massive iceberg while bound for New York.

Travel was not without great risk, even in times of peace. However, if all went well, they would be in America by mid-August, less than two weeks later. These steamships were making the crossing with increasing speed.

The family felt utterly exhausted. Yet, as they rested and pondered, Aghavni could not help but think of all that had happened since April, more than a year earlier. It seemed hard to believe that they had lost Garabed, the elder Ohanes, Nazeli, and Anush. And they even left Van, running for their lives... all in that fateful month of May. Now, some 15 months later, they were heading for America to be reunited with her eldest sons.

Hrant closed his eyes, but he was not at all sure that he would sleep, at least not right away. For now, consciously he dared to dream of what America could be like. A big part of him hoped it might look like their home in the gardens and orchards by Lake Van. He smiled. Perhaps the cities would have bustling market squares as he had previously known in their walled city. Hmmm. Would the cities have walls? Would there be electric lights as he was seeing on this beautiful ship?

"Lights out! Lights out!" A ship's attendant called out repeatedly. At ten o'clock each evening, the electric lights in steerage would be turned out. The third-class passengers had been informed that a "lights out" announcement would precede the turning out of the lights, so the passengers on these lower decks would be prepared.

Hrant could not have cared less. He was snuggled safely in their bunk with his brother and mother.

Now, all he could think about is how excited he felt at the prospect of seeing his beloved brother, Aram, again! He also looked forward to getting to know his eldest brother, Ohanes, the one the Americans called John. He could not remember much about him at all.

"We must not let ourselves look backward," Hrant reminded himself. "Papa would not want that. My sisters, my dearest Anush, would not want that."

No looking back. Time is near. Time is dear.

S.S. Kristianiafjord
Photo – Public Domain

S.S. Kristianiafjord vintage postcard
Photo – Public Domain

Time Is Now
34

MORE THAN HALF a century later, Hrant sat in his living room in New Hampshire in the United States of America. He held a framed school photograph of his second grandchild, Cassie, who had been so troubled by the dreams he recognized as originating in his youth in Armenia.

Their tutoring sessions had long ago evolved into blessed afternoons of sharing and wonderful conversation. As the weeks passed, he became more convinced than ever before that Cassie was indeed the embodiment of his dearest sister, Anush.

Hrant found it interesting that a few weeks after Cassie first revealed details of her regular nightmares, they had stopped. The bad dreams simply vanished.

The family had just celebrated Cassie's 14th birthday. The little teen would start high school that Fall.

When she suddenly announced one afternoon that the dreams had stopped and had not returned for several days, Hrant knew this was no fluke of chance.

In her analytical way, Cassie's grandmother surmised the disappearance could have been related to the fact that Cassie had finally talked them through out loud. Because they had discussed her dreams and a great deal of detail from Grampa's youth and challenges in

Armenia, it seemed utterly likely that this helped set young Cassie's heart and mind free.

Hrant had merely shaken his head. His beliefs held fast.

"No," began Hrant to Marjorie. "I do not think we found a solution in psychology. Although that sounds plausible, there is something else, something very different. I feel it in my heart."

Marjorie's face showed surprise. "What on earth do you mean, Hrant?"

"Dearest, you know I am not a believer in coincidence, right?" Marjorie nodded as her husband continued.

"I cannot tell you the exact day the unthinkable happened, and my siblings were attacked in Armenia. I can tell you it was mid-to-late April or early May. Anush had just turned 14 years of age."

Marjorie gasped. "Oh, Hrant!" Her husband gently lifted one index finger, indicating he had more to add to what he had just told her.

"Please continue, Hrant," Marjorie encouraged. She nodded to further coax him along, as she sensed a certain hesitancy.

"Dearest," Hrant began again. He paused as he reached over to place his hand on Marjorie's hand before he continued speaking.

"I have thought about this for some time. I believe that Cassie's dreams stopped on the anniversary of Anush and Nazeli's murders."

Marjorie breathed a long, heavy sigh. She could not believe that she had not thought of this herself. Of course!

It had been exactly 53 years since the Ottoman Turks' massive endeavors to obliterate the Armenians in his home city of Van. Indeed, it was in mid-to-late April or early May 1915 that Hrant's father and grandfather were ambushed and murdered by the soldiers. It was in then that his sisters had fallen victim to the same military men. And it was then that his mother, Hrant, and Vahram began their desperate run for freedom.

Everything now appeared to have fallen into place in May 1968, too. Both Cassie and Anush had early May birthdays. And yes, Cassie had just turned 14, which turned out to be the exact age at which poor Anush was killed. The parallel timing clicked in Marjorie's mind.

Now it was June. Hrant and Marjorie had previously made an important decision. They prepared for Cassie's arrival. It had been quite a year, and this was to be her final afternoon session with them.

As usual, Cassie arrived bubbling over with her latest information. Her spirited, carefree demeanor seemed to have fully returned, which pleased her grandparents greatly.

She had long ago gotten over waiting for Grampa to ask what she had learned that day in school to start each afternoon's session. She would simply step through the door and begin filling the room with that day's experiences. Today, she knew what she had to tell them would make them smile.

"It's official," Cassie announced. "I will get an 'A' for my last quarter in Algebra and be advanced to high school Geometry as a Freshman in September."

She beamed. Hrant and Marjorie's faces both lit up with smiles also. They'd harbored no doubts.

"We are so proud of you, darling," Marjorie said. "We knew you could do it."

"Remember," added Hrant. "You will always be an 'A' student whenever you choose to be. I did not have to teach you anything."

"Not true!" Cassie protested immediately. "You taught me everything. I could not have... well... I *would* not have succeeded without your help and love. Both of you! I love you both so much!"

Cassie's voice grew soft as she continued. "Thank you for believing in me and my abilities, even when I did not believe in myself. Your patience and understanding are amazing."

"We will always believe in you, dear," added Marjorie. Then she looked at Hrant. "Is it time?" He nodded.

"Yes," Hrant said aloud. "The time is now."

Marjorie reached behind a cushion on the sofa where they sat. She had carefully placed a small, clear, plastic box there before Cassie arrived.

Then Hrant continued speaking. His delivery exuded the calm, thoughtful, and measured manner Cassie had grown to love.

"For all possible reasons, both known to us and beyond our knowledge, you have always been our most Armenian grandchild. Your grandmother and I have talked about this at length, Cassie. We want you to have the only thing I have from Armenia. Please accept my mother's wedding ring as our gift of love to you."

Hrant and Marjorie smiled softly as they watched Cassie's mouth gape. She slowly extended her hands to accept the precious box.

"So, Great Grammy's ring *did* make it to America! You had not mentioned it, so I had not dared to ask. I... I don't think I would ever dare to wear it," Cassie uttered. "I would be too scared that something would happen to it, or I might lose it!"

"I understand exactly what you mean," began her grandmother. "It is pure gold. Thus, the metal is very soft for a ring. I did not dare to wear it either, for those same reasons. I, too, feared that I might damage this precious keepsake."

Now Marjorie reached over and showed Cassie how to open the box, revealing the treasured family heirloom. "You see, Grampa put it on a chain for me. I did wear it around my neck for a time. But I still worried, so I eventually stopped wearing it at all."

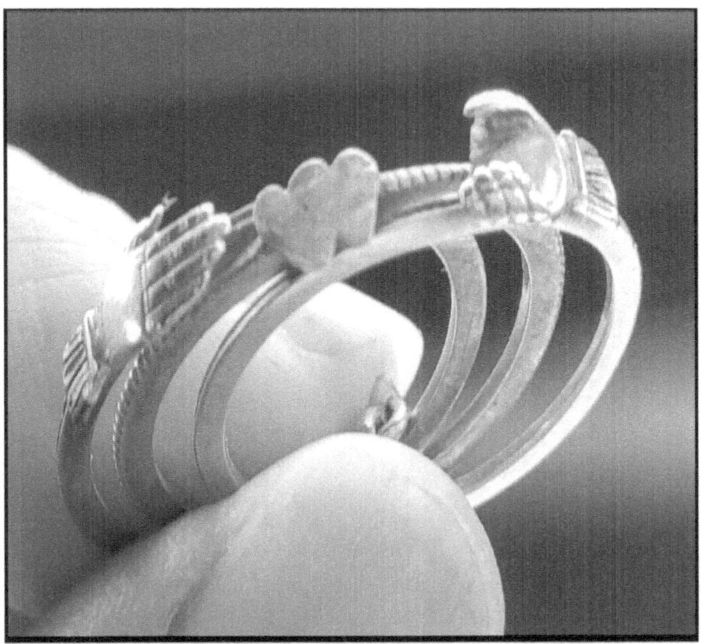

Aghavni Gulumian's wedding ring
Author's personal photo

Grampa added, "Back when your mother was born, your grandmother and I went through some severe, financially challenging times during the Great Depression. But your grandmother remained true to her word. Just as my mother did, Grammy had vowed to never sell the ring for any reason."

Cassie immediately echoed the sentiments. "Oh, Grammy! Grampa! I hope you know that I would *never* sell this ring. Absolutely never! I would let myself starve first! I will treasure and guard it. I honor this ring for all it represents of Great Grammy and you! Of all our family. Of Armenia. Of sacrifice. Of perseverance!"

"We knew you had the right heart to hold this treasure of our Armenian family," Hrant added. "We always knew."

The loving grandparents now removed the ring and chain from the little box. They showed Cassie the delicate trio of rings that folded open from the one triple band. They opened the clasped hands, revealing the joined hearts in the center and the three actual gold rings.

Hrant gently picked up the chain with the ring on it. He carefully fastened it around Cassie's neck.

"Today you wear this ring," he said. "Mama would be proud of you. I believe she smiles now that her treasure is safely in the hands of another generation."

"I promise to treasure it always," Cassie said. "And someday, I will seek out some special way to share exactly how precious this ring is, along with all it represents from your homeland."

Hrant and Marjorie hugged their granddaughter. He offered one final thought.

"You will know when the time is right and what to do with your Armenian great grandmother's dear wedding ring. For now, just continue trying to do your best in school, in church, in the community, and in your family. Do not let fear control you or hold you back. Find comfort in the fact that your destiny may well be found in some reflection of your dreams, even dreams you may not have yet dreamed."

That night Cassie fell asleep amidst a whirlwind of thoughts and images. She felt rather overwhelmed by a sense of serious responsibility to preserve this precious gift, this Armenian treasure. She envisioned her great-grandparents. She then imagined the thousands... the hundreds of thousands... no... the millions of people symbolized in the ring, and the shared history that now trickled down to future generations.

A solitary tear slid down her cheek. Cassie brimmed with history and family and emotion. She felt deeply humbled and considered herself immeasurably honored by her new responsibility, whether it was justifiable or not.

One ring represented so much. The love. The challenges. The perseverance.

Cassie even felt peculiar gratitude for those horrid nightmares she had endured. Those bad dreams had led her to all this learning and shared love with her grandparents.

She drifted off to sleep. Her last conscious thoughts reminded her that, indeed, time is dear.

Hrant and Marjorie Gulumian
Gulumian family photo

Final Note

WHEN THE *DESTINY* story continues, young Hrant grows up, experiencing new encounters, questions, and discrimination in his new land. He, like so many other displaced Armenians, feels grateful to be alive, but mightily challenged to forge a positive path and establish family roots. Then comes a shocking revelation that changes everything for the next generation of Gulumian descendants.

Photo courtesy of David Peterson

Invitation:

Thank you for reading ***Destiny of Dreams: Time Is Dear***, a true labor of love for the author. If you enjoyed the book, please consider leaving a brief review on Amazon or elsewhere so others can receive the same value you have. Honest reviews help her write even better books for you and others to enjoy. Thank you!

Historic Timetable

For some historical perspective, we include some dates of relative and interesting information.

3500 BC

Earliest recorded history of Armenians, the Hayasa-Azzi tribes (a.k.a. Proto-Armenians), the indigenous people of Eastern Anatolia Armenian Highlands.

Circa 2,000 BC

Armenian ancestors are known to have lived around Lake Van at base of Mount Ararat in Caucasus Mountains.

1300 BC

Iron Age - Urartu becomes first kingdom in Armenia.

1100 BC

The highly advanced kingdom of Ararat (a.k.a. Urartu) forms its capital in Tushpa (a.k.a. Van).

585 BC

Median army captures city of Van, causing the fall of the Urartian kingdom.

189 BC

Armenian Empire reaches its greatest size under Tigran the Great.

301 AD

Armenian King Tiridates III declares Christianity the official religion, making Armenia the first Christian nation in the world.

428

Armenia comes under Persian and Byzantine rule.

921

Cathedral of the Holy Cross is built on Akhtamar Island, Lake Van's 2nd largest island.

15th Century

Ottoman Empire absorbs Armenia.

1825

U.S. Navy conducts anti-piracy operations in the Aegean Sea, which was, at the time, controlled by the Ottomans.

1831

United States sends first formal envoy to the Ottoman Empire.

1850

Emin Bey makes first Ottoman visit to U.S.

1855

May – first Ottoman honorary consulate opens in United States.

1858

Patrick Joseph "PJ" Kennedy is born in Massachusetts in USA. All 4 of his grandparents had immigrated to U.S. in 1840s to escape the Irish famine. As an Irish Catholic, he found himself excluded from upper-class activities; he became an East Boston pub owner & politician. The owner of 3 saloons, he served in the MA House of Representatives and was the grandfather of President John F. Kennedy.

1863

01/01 Ottoman Empire issued its first adhesive postage stamp. (The USA had switched to adhesive postage stamps on July 1, 1847.)

1870

Garabed Ohanes Gulumian is born in Van, Armenia. (Mis-noted as 1868 elsewhere.) He was the 2nd son of Ohanes Argistis Gulumian.

1871

Aghavni Gadara Samargian was born in Salmas, Armenia, near the Persian border, in modern-day Iran. She was the 2nd daughter of Ara and Gadara (Movsesian) Samargian.

1880

Ottomans set up Consulate-General Office in NYC to monitor anti-Ottoman Armenian activity in the USA.

1885

Automobile invented, but roads in Armenia are not yet built for cars.

Grigor Terlemezian assists Mekertich Portukalian (later called the "Father of the Armenian Patriotic Society of Europe") to form the Armenakan Party. This underground organization against the ruling system merged in 1921 into the Armenian Democratic Liberal Party.

1887

Garabed Ohanes Gulumian marries Aghavni Gadara Samargian.

The Social Democrat Hunchakian Party is formed by a group of Armenian students in Geneva, Switzerland. It is the oldest, continually operating Armenian political party and the first socialist party to operate in the Ottoman Empire and Persia (now Iran).

1888

11/08   Ohanes Garabed Gulumian born to Garabed and Aghavni Gulumian, becoming their firstborn.

09/06   Joseph Patrick Kennedy, Sr. born to Patrick Joseph "PJ" and Mary Kennedy. Born and raised in

East Boston, he became a noted businessman, investor, and politician. Married to Rose Kennedy, he made his fortune in the stock market. The patriarch of the Irish American political family, his son John F. Kennedy became President of the United States.

1893

11/28   Aram Garabed Gulumian, their 2nd son, is born to Garabed and Aghavni.

1895 – 1896

Ottoman orders from Constantinople direct Turkish and Kurdish forces to systematically attack Armenian quarters in cities and Armenian villages, killing more than 200,000 Armenians in what became known as the Hamidian Massacres.

1898

03/26 Vahram Garabed and twin sister Nazeli Gulumian born to Garabed and Aghavni.

1900

Van city population reaches 40,000 (adult male citizens), with Armenians comprising an overwhelming majority. The city featured 12 Armenian churches, all of which were blown to bits by the Turks in 1915.

The Vilayet (Province) of Van is noted for its population of nearly 400,000 (male citizens) and covering 15,000 square miles, connecting Persia with Russia. Amongst the nearly 400 villages and towns, popular were beekeeping for honey, plus wine and tobacco production. The region was rich with hot springs, petroleum springs, gold, coal, copper, lime, salt, and more.

1901

05/01 Anush Gulumian born to Garabed and Aghavni.

1906

03/06   Hrant Garabed Gulumian born to Garabed and Aghavni, their 4th & youngest son.

04/15 The Armenian General Benevolent Union (AGBU), a non-profit Armenian organization, is founded in Cairo, Egypt to contribute to the spiritual and cultural development of the Armenian people.

The United States upgrades its presence in Constantinople with an official embassy.

Although there is, as yet, no official consulate office in Norway, H.D. Peirce is appointed as the first United States Ambassador to Norway. (Before this, a representative was based in Stockholm and covered several nations.

1908

The Young Turk Revolution removes Sultan Abdul Hamid II from power in the Ottoman Empire.

1909

Ottoman presence in Washington, DC is designated as an embassy. (Remained until Ottomans severed diplomatic relations with the United States after U.S. declared war against Germany April 4, 1917.)

11/09   Ohanes Garabed Gulumian departs Patras, on the Greek island of Crete aboard the Oceania, bound for New York City.

11/24 Ohanes Garabed Gulumian (erroneously spelled Ohanes Giloumian and Gielumian on ship's manifest) arrives at Ellis Island in U.S.

11/25   Ohanes Garabed Gulumian goes to 79 Heard Street in Boston, MA, joining an Uncle Krikor Baudukian (or Boudakian).   Ohanes was 21 years old.

1910

Ottomans set up a second Consulate-General Office in the USA. This one in Boston is to monitor Armenians in USA.

1912

04/10   Titanic sets sail for France from Southampton, England.

04/11   Titanic makes last scheduled stop in Europe at Queenstown, Ireland, now called Cobh.

04/14-15 Titanic sinks in North Atlantic after striking massive iceberg.

06/30 Aram Garabed Gulumian departs from Patras, Greece aboard the ship, Martha Washington, traveling in steerage and listing his occupation as a teacher.

08/13 Aram arrives in United States, joining his brother, Ohanes, at 907 Broadway in Chelsea, MA.

September - Aram Gulumian begins studying toward an advanced education degree at Bridgewater State University in Massachusetts.

1913

1913 - 1916 Henry Morgenthau, US Ambassador to Ottoman Empire, holds high-level meetings with Turkish leaders and calling for a stop to the official persecution of and increasing attacks on Armenians.

07/16 Ohanes Garabed Gulumian officially files his petition in Boston to become naturalized U.S. citizen.

1913 - 1921 Albert G. Schmedeman serves as US Ambassador to Norway.

1914

01/31 Armenian Evangelical Union of Ararat is formed and based in Yerevan.

The Armenian Patriarch of Constantinople presents a list of 2,549 sacred places under his supervision... 200 monasteries & 1600 churches. (Note: By 1974 only 916 Armenian churches could be identified within Turkish borders, half of which were almost destroyed, with only crumbled ruins of 252 remaining.)

07/28 The Great War, later called World War 1, begins.

08/01 Young Turks enter Great War on the side of the Central Powers by signing the Secret Ottoman-German Alliance.

August - Turks abruptly start closing Armenian schools in Diyarbakir and Harpout (and other areas) to use them as military barracks. Armenian families begin holding classes in their homes.

Fall and Winter - Turks call all able-bodied young Armenian men to serve in Turkish army.

Fall, 1914 - On the streets, Armenians stop wearing colors red, white, and blue together as Turks felt that showed Armenians favored the Turks' war enemies.

09/14 The Tatiana Committee is established by Her Highness Grand Duchess Tatiana Nikolaevna (daughter of Tsar Nicholas II). The committee provides financial assistance for refugees, helps in resettlement, registration, tracking relatives, arranging employment, and providing meal stations and hospitals.

Aram Gulumian joins Alpha Chapter of Kappa Delta Phi fraternity at Bridgewater State University. (Aram is on the Alumni list in the 1950 The Golden Year of Kappa Delta Phi publication, which recognizes

Bridgewater as the first chapter of this fraternity, founded on April 14, 1900.)

1915

01/12 Talaat Bey Pasha, Minister of the Interior, declares there is only room for Turks in Turkey.

January - US Ambassador Henry Morgenthau reports that Christians in Ottoman Empire are in great peril.

February - Ottoman Turks carry out first wave of Armenian "deportations."

Armenian women and girls start covering themselves with black headscarves and shawls, even to go to church. Although non-Muslim women had not previously been required to do so, they do anything to not annoy the Turks.

March - Some Armenian men close their shops and start working from home to avoid contact with Ottoman enforcers.

04/01   Mass arrest of Armenian political leaders begins in the six Armenian provinces.

04/02   General robbery & arrests of Armenians begins occurring throughout Bitlis & Erzurum provinces. In the Sivas province, Ottoman battalions begin regular attacks on Armenian villages and increase brutality.

04/03 Mass arrests and searches for weapons take place in the Armenian cities of Marash and Hadjin, with seizure of all arms, including household knives. Many rapes are reported.

04/08   Famous monastery of Zeitun is burned by the Young Turks' forces.

04/09   Young Turks declare mandatory meeting in the city of Marash. The sole purpose is to deport Armenians, and the Turkish government forbids any civilian defensive action.

04/11   Talaat Pasha tells Armenian parliamentary there will be no massacres.

04/12   Widespread attacks & looting of Armenian villages in Bitlis & Erzurum provinces.

04/14   Governor-General of Van, Tahir Jevdet, invites Armenian parliamentary deputies from Van & Dashnak leader Ishkhan to a conference.

04/15   Armenian refugees from villages surrounding the city of Van arrive and notify Van's inhabitants that at least 80 villages in the Van province have already been obliterated. Reports show that at least 24,000 Armenians there have been slaughtered over 3 days.

04/16   Armenian leaders Vramian and Ishkhan are slain during the night in the Kurdish village of Hirj by chetes (the Pasha's killing parties) on orders from Governor-General Tahir Jevdet.

04/17   Friendly Kurds inform Van's inhabitants of the assassinations of Vramian and Ishkhan.

Mid-April - The ambush & executions of Garabed Gulumian and his father, Ohanes Gulumian take place outside walled city of Van.

Mid-April - The attack and shootings of Nazeli Gulumian (age 17) and Anush Gulumian (age 14) takes place at their home in Van, Armenia.

Mid-April - Aghavni G. Gulumian escapes from Van with her two youngest sons, Vahram and Hrant.

04/18 – 04/30 Another 32,000 Armenians are slaughtered in villages of the Van province, including remote villages.

04/18 Governor-General of Van demands all Armenians in the city of Van surrender their weapons. The Armenians refuse, because of the attacks on the surrounding villages. Their resistance is called "revolutionary."

Armenian resistance against Ottoman Turks officially begins in Van, Armenia, marking one of the only acts of self-defense against Ottoman Empire in the Armenian genocide.

04/19 House-by-house searches are made in province of Diyarbakir with reports of widespread persecution taking place.

04/20 Zeitun deportation of 25,000 Armenians.

Upon order of the Governor-General Reshid, the first large-scale arrests of Armenians take place in Diyarbakir.

Twenty Armenian Social Democratic Hunchakian Party members are brought to the Central Prison in Constantinople to face court-martial. (They are later hanged publicly on June 2, 1915.)

04/24 Two hundred and fifty Armenian intellectuals and community leaders are arrested in Constantinople. Most are later executed. Some are sent to prison in Chankri and Ayash, where they are later slain. (This date is listed by most as the official start of the Armenian Genocide that lasted until 1917.)

Staff of "Azadamart", the leading Armenian newspaper in Constantinople, are arrested. On June 15th they are slain in Diyarbakir, where they had been transported & imprisoned.

04/25-04/26   Various incidents of the hanging of Armenians and abuse of women are reported.

Under direction from the Young Turks' leadership, large-scale Armenian deportations begin, and 1.5 - 2 million Armenians are systematically massacred in what later becomes known as the world's first genocide.

04/27 Twenty-six Armenian leaders are arrested in Marsovan. A two-week search for weapons begins, along with many acts of violence and the abuse of women.

04/29   Russian citizens of Armenian origin are arrested in Constantinople.

The disarming of Armenians in Constantinople begins, amidst many acts of violence.

04/30 The Vice-Governor of Erzincan begins the persecution of Armenians with the arrest of many intellectuals.

05/01   The arrest of Armenian professors and teachers at the American Euphrates College in Kharput begins.

05/02   Halil Pasha's forces are defeated by the Russian Army in the Caucasus. The Turkish troops retreat to Van, Bitlis, and Mush, where they participate in the massacres of Armenians.

05/24   A joint declaration by the Allied Powers (namely Great Britain, France, and Russia) accuses the Young Turk regime of crimes against humanity and civilization.

05/30 Russians declare a Republic of Van and appoint Aram Manukian as Governor.   (The fledgling city republic only lasts 2 months.)

07/31 The Russians leave Van for other fronts in the Great War. Turkish forces sweep through the city, and Van is lost. The new republic is doomed, and Van is destroyed.

George Horton, former US Consul General at Smyrna, writes in a report to US Secretary of State, "I wish to repeat that the consistent policy of the Turk, since the fall of Abdul Hamid, has been the expulsion, killing, and extermination of the Christian races."

1916

June - Aram Gulumian graduates from Bridgewater State University.

08/06 Aghavni, Vahram, and Hrant Gulumian depart from Kristiania, Norway aboard the Kristianiafjord, bound for New York City.

References, Resources & Further Reading

Cornell University; www.Guides.library.cornell.edu
Gulumian, M.R. and Martin, C.B. (2013)
    Of the Same Blood: Your Eurasian Heritage.
    Quiet Thunder Publishing
Holocaust Museum Houston; www.HMH.org
International Association of Genocide Scholars
Liberty Ellis Island Foundation
Radio Free Europe Radio Liberty; RFERL.org
United States Holocaust Memorial Museum

www.Encyclopedia.USHMM.org
www.Ancient.eu/MountArarat/
www.ArmenianEagle.com
www.Armenian-Genocide.org
www.BBC.com
www.Courses.LumenLearning.com
www.DoSomething.org
www.EchoesAndReflections.org
www.EN.Wikipedia.org
www.EuroNews.com
www.EyewitnessToHistory.com/
www.ArmenianMassacre.htm
www.FacingHistory.org
www.Genocide1915.org
www.Genocide-Museum.am
www.GreekCityTimes.com

www.Heritage.StatueOfLiberty.org
www.History.com
www.HistoryPlace.com
www.NationalArchives.gov.UK
www.NationalGeographic.com
www.NewYorker.com
www.NPR.org
www.NYTimes.com
www.NZHistory.govt.nz
www.Reuters.com
www.Stanford.edu/Armenia
www.Surface.syr.edu
www.Telegraph.co.UK
www.WHC.UNESCO.org
www.WilsonCenter.org
www.WSJ.com

Additional Photography Credits

Page
Front Cover   Gulumian family
8   Manchester Union Leader; CB Martin
9, 251, 254   Burnham / Gulumian family
Back Cover   Krikor Abo; Claire Johnson

About the Author

Cathy Burnham Martin's first published work came at age 6 when an early poem won a town library contest. Back then, her parents refused to let her have the then-popular Chatty Cathy doll, stating that one chatty Cathy in the house was more than enough. Though poetry took a back seat, she drove her writing and blabbing proficiencies along a highly eclectic career path through college recruitment, telecom corporate communications, TV broadcasting with an ABC affiliate, station management of an award-winning PEG-access station, bank organizing, marketing, and investor relations. An active board member and volunteer, she received Easter Seals' David P. Goodwin Lifetime Commitment Award.

This professional voiceover artist, humorist, corporate communications geek, musical actress, journalist, and dedicated foodie earned numerous awards as a news anchor and businesswoman. She produced and hosted groundbreaking documentaries, TV specials, and news reports, from the Moscow Superpower Summit and the opening of the Berlin Wall to coverage of Presidential Primaries.

A born storyteller and business speaker, Cathy remains a member of Actors Equity and writes articles for the GoodLiving123.com website.

Other Titles
by Cathy Burnham Martin

Good Living Skills: Learned from My Mother

Encouragement: How to Be and Find the Best

The Bimbo Has Brains... and Other Freaky Facts

The Bimbo Has MORE Brains...
    Surviving Political Correctness

A Dangerous Book for Dogs: Train Your Humans

Dog Days in the Life of the Miles-Mannered Man

Healthy Thinking Habits: Seven Attitude Skills Simplified

Of the Same Blood: Your Eurasian Heritage

Sage, Thyme & Other Life Seasonings: Perspectives

Fifty Years of Fabulous Family Favorites, Volumes 1-3

Champagne! Facts, Fizz, Food & Fun

Dockside Dining, Volumes 1-3

Cranberry Cooking

Lobacious Lobster

The Communication Coach:
    Business Communication Tips from the Pros

See all works from Cathy Burnham Martin
www.GoodLiving123.com

Partial List of Audiobooks Narrated by Cathy Burnham Martin

<u>Fiction</u>

A Dangerous Book for Dogs –
    Train Your Humans with the Bandit Method
Kremlins Trilogy (Violent content warning)
    Citadels of Fire
    Bastions of Blood
    Dungeons of Destiny:
        An Epic Russian Historical Romance
Daniel's Fork: A Mystery Set in the Daniel's Fork
        Universe (Adult content warning)
The Relentless Brit

<u>Non-Fiction</u>

Encouragement: How to Be and Find the Best
Healthy Thinking Habits:
    Seven Attitude Skills Simplified
The Bimbo Has Brains: And Other Freaky Facts
The Bimbo Has MORE Brains:
    Surviving Political Correctness
31 Days to a Stronger Marriage: A Guide to Building
    Closer Relationships
Exploring Past Lives: A Guide to the Soul's Travels
Why We Fail in Love: A Study into the Pursuit of
    One of Mankind's Most Precious Desires
The Hormone Fix:
    Naturally Rebalance Your System in 10 Weeks

www.ingramcontent.com/pod-product-compliance
Lightning Source LLC
Chambersburg PA
CBHW030859060726
47591CB00005B/1342